The Gathering Thread

Book One of the "Threads of Fate" Trilogy

Stephen P. Radford

Copyright © 2018 Stephen P. Radford

All rights reserved. No part of this work may be reproduced in any form, by any method, without express written permission from the author.

This is a work of fiction. Names, characters, places and incidents are the product of the author's imagination or are used fictitiously. Any similarity to real persons, living or dead, business establishments, events or locations are entirely coincidental.

http://stephenradford.com

ISBN-13: 978-1718783638
ISBN-10: 1718783639

For Kathryn

You have always turned small steps
into greater strides.

Thank you for believing.

ACKNOWLEDGMENTS

Special thanks go to Jill Fitterling for graciously dotting the i's and crossing the t's.

Thank you Lauren T. Hart for shifting the gears and activating the business side of my brain.

To the Hill People: If I could count the ways, there'd be 71. Thank you all for the inspirational interludes whilst writing this book. #holdme

1

SADY NA SKALCE, PRAGUE, CZECHOSLOVAKIA

WINTER 1952

Jiri and Karel scrambled across the west side of the park where trees were clustered tightly. Ground fog had risen and settled over the quiet city of Prague after a long and arduous winter. This morning, the chill had reached dew point. The lack of visibility, however, gave the two twelve-year-olds an advantage. They had to keep their profiles low, especially now that both boys were far enough away from their school grounds to be considered truants.

The mid-morning roads were getting busier with slow, trundling, snow-covered automobiles. This meant that there was less chance for anybody to stop should they be in the position to spot the two mischievous miscreants. It was any adult's duty to report such an act – something of an unwritten law. But in the depth of winter, stopping a car engine once you had it running was a pointless exercise. It may have been the right time to get away with truancy, but still, these were times of zero tolerance. There were many other ways by which truants could be caught. For Jiri, this was his first time playing in such a dangerous game, led by the carefree attitude of Karel - whom did not care for rules, and for the most part, had very little regard for having (let alone using) a moral compass. Nothing was more important than spending time smoking, and drinking while staring over his handcrafted fishing line that dangled over the mighty Vltava River. Karel's uncle owned a fishing boat on the west side of the river, and on a Friday, he was never there.

'He smokes the strongest tobacco,' Karel boasted. He took a moment to catch a breath behind a park supply shed. 'You wait until you taste his red vodka. Gives you balls of steel. Well, that's what Onkel Aldo says anyway.'

Jiri nodded enthusiastically as Karel laughed off being unfit and out of breath.

'C'mon!' Karel said as he bounded for the main street, exposed and at risk. He and Jiri ducked behind a slow-moving Tatra 600, and then darted into a narrow back alley, through into the back gardens of the side street that ran parallel to the main road. Together they weaved in and around overflowing snow-covered garbage bins.

A litter of dogs barked at them. Karel ignored them, but Jiri's hesitation earned him their full attention and bloodthirsty rebuke, for he was a stranger in their territory. Jiri's guilt stopped him in his tracks. He hadn't the stomach for wrongdoing or regrets. The first word he ever learnt in school was "následek" which was the common Czech word for "consequence". Naturally they learnt the same word in Latin, German and Russian just to ensure that every child carried a crystal-clear understanding on those first days of orientation.

Coming out of the back street, they finally reached the bend in the main road that ran along the Vltava River. This road was quiet enough, but the two boys still had to cross it without being seen. Karel did his best to approach the street looking taller than he ever could be, with his head down into his poorly-fitted jacket, and his cap dipped enough so that nobody could see the whites of his eyes. His swagger sealed the deal – at least in his mind – that he was just a common street Joe heading to work. Jiri followed on behind and adopted the same stature, stance, and swagger. However, he couldn't hide his roaming sense of suspicion as two cars passed. A horse-drawn milk cart caught up alongside them, and in the same moment, the driver of the milk cart shouted at the top of his raspy lungs, 'stoy!'

The desired instruction - which effectively

caused the horse to halt - triggered a sudden hot flush of panic for the two boys who may as well have been unbroken wild horses reacting to a starter pistol for the first time in their lives.

'Run!' Karel blasted over his shoulder. He took up high strides along the snow and ice-capped street. A chain-link fence stretched alongside the pathway, giving no chance for them to make a break for cover. More houses up ahead, and a gap between the chain-linked fences finally presented itself. Karel sped down the gap, down the side-alley as fast as his could. Jiri had only made it to the gap in the fence when he heard the sound of brakes screeching along the main road.

He knew he'd been spotted.

He chose in that moment not to follow Karel any further. He turned to serve his punishment, locking eyes with the driver who was already out of his vehicle. The man reached for the back door of the car and opened it.

Out of breath, and completely defeated, Jiri slowly walked to the passenger door of his father's dark brown Skoda 1200. As he took his seat, his father closed the door, and without saying a word, headed back to the gap in the fence to give one final glance down the pathway where Karel had escaped. Satisfied that he was only leaving with one runaway today, Nikolai Ivanov returned to the driver's seat. Nikolai lit a small cigar and put on his black leather driving gloves. On the seat beside him was his private notebook, complete with its Frenchmanufactured ballpoint BIC pen - together with his hat and service revolver, along with his badge of honour for the StB - the state security for the SNB police force.

Nikolai was a highly decorated and respected officer with an earned right to work in plain civilian clothes, unlike the other police division, the VB, who worked to represent a visible show of force. They weren't there to blend in nor were they entitled to the authority, nor the autonomy of the StB.

It took him a few turns to get the engine started. The thaw at least was on his side today.

'Jiri,' His father said as he pulled away from the kerbside. 'You are not well.'

Jiri looked up and frowned. 'Father, I shouldn't have done what I did... I'm...'

'Be quiet when I'm talking to you.' Nikolai said without raising his voice.

Jiri buried his head once more into his jacket and waited for his father to continue.

'It is my fortune that I saw you both on the other side of the park. I won't take you back to school today. You know I cannot leave you at home. I have to be at work now.' He then reiterated. 'It is important for you to remember: today, you are not well.'

Jiri said nothing for a few cold foggy breaths. His father looked at him through the rear-view mirror. That heavy feeling was being observed. Jiri couldn't shrink down any further with guilt and his father knew that. He needed his son to be on side. It was important that he didn't push him away...

'However...' Nikolai maintained his serious disposition; however, he did have something to offer, 'when you return to school, not tomorrow, but on Monday, I will have to give you a note for physical education; you will be too weak, but you will watch instead, or be excused for library duties. Is that clear?'

Jiri tried hard not to smile. Jiri hated gymnastics and sports, and was always more of a library worm. He could see the familiar creases pulling on the outer edges of his father's eyes, which meant that he too was struggling to keep from breaking a smile.

Oh for sure, for Nikolai, it was far more important to protect than to punish. It was more important to be on Jiri's level than to be the overlord and ram the rulebook down his throat whenever it was required. Nikolai needed Jiri to also be there for his mother while he himself had to work, often late but rarely through the night. Jiri was also discouraged from making contact with her when she was at her worst, and acted more like a centurion guarding her door, ensuring it was closed and not open to opportunity. It was important that nobody came into contact with her, when the darkness fell.

When it came to the communist red cloud that had smothered them in their post-war lives, there was no certainty, no perks for position, and no choice but to keep your family clean in the eyes of the people. There was always risk of putting that belief ahead of family itself, and push the nearest and dearest right to the edge of tolerance. After all, fear could easily rule over all if you gave it an inch.

On the bad days, Nikolai would have to be both mother and the father to their son. He was the educator, protector, housekeeper and the one who put the literal and proverbial bread on the table. He came from a strong Slovak family that also branched into German lineage. Still, Nikolai carried a position of power, and that itself gave him leverage when needed. He had to ensure that his Italian born wife and their son had a grounded and stable life amongst the Czech people – most of who had already gone through enough, what with the German Occupation, and were finally reaching towards stability in their own lives – under tight Soviet control. Life was delicate, however decidedly better than the most recent alternative.

Jiri's mother, Patricia, came from an Italian/Jewish family who had been brought up within a Venetian ghetto. It was savage, brutal and near fatal circumstances that brought Nikolai and Patricia together. The Ivanov's had a unique ability in the area of "finding things". Since the moment he met Patricia, together, their abilities to know things through precognition had soon gotten very strong.

Patricia was said to have been a lucky one, having avoided the cull that the German army had enforced on any man, woman, or child of Jewish descent. Being with Nikolai gave her a protection that she felt she could never live up to. If nobody else could have it, she felt that she didn't deserve it.

The trauma from these past event meant that Patricia suffered from severe bouts of mental depression. While Nikolai worked during the day, she spent most of her time creating Venetian masks, clothing, music boxes, toys, and other trinkets indicative of her homeland of Italy in the privacy of their apartment, within the suburban regions of Prague.

Jiri was kept in the dark about the family history, and knew only that he was a vital part of keeping her sane. During those bad weeks that lasted forever, Patricia would make and box items ready for Jiri to take to the weekend market. This he did automatically, with or without her help. On good days, as rare as they were, it was as if they were a family again.

One day, Jiri will be told everything. The whole family history is still something of a mystery to nearly everybody except Nikolai and Patricia. As far as Jiri knew, she fell in love with Nikolai when they met on vacation in Italy. Half-truths are easier to remember. He was aware about her creative background, and that she once made gifts and home comforts that were Italia-inspired. That was truth enough.

His father said he was Prague-born, but Jiri did not want to believe that. The men he knew around him were hardly role models, and nothing about them reflected any aspect his father's character. As far as Jiri was concerned, Nikolai came from a place of mystery, where heroes are born and were sent here to be the example. Beyond Jiri's ideas that stemmed from an overactive imagination, the family history remained as cloudy as the fog that settled thick and heavy on that winter morning.

One day, he will ask. He will ask about everything and on that day, it will be as if he'd always known.

2

U SMALTOVNY RESIDENTIAL DISTRICT

TWENTY MINUTES LATER

Nikolai pulled up at a tall mustard-coloured apartment building in the northern residential quarter of Prague. Through the window, Jiri saw many black coats sharply contrasting against the white snow – which was now once again, falling silently, steadily, and covering the shoulders of the uniformed VB officers who gathered in front of the apartment steps. A small handful of onlookers, rubber-neckers mainly, stood staring. They talked amongst each other, making up their own stories as to what had happened inside that apartment on the fourth floor, as if they were watching street theatre. The police didn't care for their passing glances into the apartment foyer, but kept them far enough away behind old rickety sawhorse stands.

Nikolai turned around and reminded Jiri that he had to stay down, out of sight while he went up to do his job. He left Jiri with a blanket and his spun-aluminium soup thermos. Normally, Nikolai would never go without food on days like this, but he was sure that Jiri would need soup more than he. At any time, he could easily jostle one of his own men to get him something else later in the day.

Jiri nodded and reached for a blanket that would give him the cover and the warmth that he needed while he waited. The chill on his forehead made it easy for him to look strained and unwell.

He watched his father walk over to his comrades, waving his notebook in his hand. He towered over them in height, despite being a tad thinner in build. What Jiri's father lacked in bulk, he had in character. Many officers made the effort to shake his hand before he'd had the chance to venture into the darkness of the apartment atrium. What went on beyond that point - from Jiri's point of view at least - was left to his imagination.

Jiri wiped a clear streak across the window with his sleeve which made it easier for him to watch one of the plain clothed StB officers, Nikolai's irritable tag-along, Pavel Fleischaker, as he made his way through the barriers. Pavel was a burly man whose weight was reflected in his slow-grinding eye movement. He wouldn't move a muscle for anyone if it weren't for those eyes. They worked overtime, clocking, staring down and more often than not, they made a clear-cut case for aggressive intimidation. To Jiri, he was a bully. Jiri never liked it when he visited Nikolai at their home. He always wanted Jiri to get out of sight the moment he arrived so that he could play buddy-buddy with his work colleague. That way, Pavel could cuss without having "little pecker pasta shell ears" listening in.

As Pavel stood on the steps of the apartment smoking a cigarette, there was a moment of familiar paranoia that forced him to direct his view straight to Nikolai's car. Jiri felt he could stare his way through the cold steel of the car door and through that blanket, right at him where he sat. Pavel didn't want that little half-Italian Jew reading into him, whether he was there in the car or not. As Pavel squinted and looked long and hard at Nikolai's car, Jiri looked away and hid.

His little pasta shell ears were burning.

There were moments alone with Pavel when Jiri realized that he had an issue around kids which made him uncomfortable. To Nikolai's face, he would just be kidding around, but when nobody was looking, Pavel would indicate that there was nothing but animosity. There was no need for words however. The 'throat cut' gesture was usually all he needed to put the message across to the boy.

Jiri wiped along his window as he tracked Pavel

along. Pavel had set his sights on a weary man riding a bicycle. The man carried far too many goods, which overflowed within a wooden crate on his lap, and he was obviously struggling to keep it together as he peddled along the cobbled road. Pavel flicked away his butt and headed over to the man, stopping him in his path. Jiri couldn't hear what was being said, but he had an eye for reading lips. Pavel asked the thin-faced man for identification cards. In a panicked fumble, the man let go of a jar of preserved jam. The jar smashed against the ground. Its contents plummeted into a mound of sticky mess. The papers were finally produced and Jiri watched Pavel's lips mouth, 'Coho - Delivery job? Your boss has you down as a fucking pack mule.' Pavel waved his thumb, telling the very silent, very still biker to get going. The poor man gave no resistance, but it was clear in his eyes that a little piece of his pride and dignity had smashed on the ground along with that glass jar.

Pavel looked down at the smashed mess on the road for a moment before looking about for a uniformed VB officer. Somebody who wasn't doing anything important whom could clean up the mess. Sure enough, one of the officers got caught in Pavel's web and received quick and concise verbal instructions. Before leaving to find the tools to clean the mess, Pavel troubled the young officer for a smoke. Pavel lit up, looked directly at Nikolai's car. Pavel lowered his head enough to make the sincerest of all dagger eyes. He removed his cigarette from his mouth and spat out mucus onto the road before heading back into the apartment for another attempt at serious detective work.

Jiri breathed a sigh of relief. The look in Pavel's eye was telling, and he had a strong feeling that he could sense his presence. Jiri was almost certain that he could see through steel. Pavel could see through anything if he put his mind to it. Especially if he knew that there was a possibility that Jiri was on the other side.

3

U SMALTOVNY RESIDENTIAL DISTRICT

TWO HOURS LATER

Restlessness.

Jiri couldn't feel his fingers. Only the uniformed officers standing outside of the apartment could empathize, even though they had the luxury of plunging their glove-covered hands into deep, serviceable pockets. Jiri's coat had shallow pockets and as for gloves, he'd lost every pair he'd been given. He reached into his father's storage compartment, just in case there was a spare pair for him to wear, but alas, his father travelled far too light to think about bringing extra for passengers. Jiri felt his nose itch with discomfort.

Enough was enough.

Jiri would rather be at home and still be in the

good mind to stay out of the way of his mother. There he could remain hidden away in his room where it was warm under his patchwork quilt. Surely his father would understand that. The inside of that apartment complex would be warmer and it was in reach of him, right there, and right now.

Jiri didn't take a second thought. He opened the car door and slammed it shut. He walked tall and strong, playing up the signature role as the son of the respected StB officer. He was untouchable. That all changed when one of the VB policemen called after him as he headed through into the foyer. A group of heavy coats and hats obscured his view. Jiri pinned himself against the wall until he could see the staircase. He spotted a man in a suit – an old StB officer Jiri thought – filing alongside the already dense crowd of long coats. Jiri saw the space behind the VB policeman and bolted up the staircase. He paused only when his feet touched down on the landing for each floor. He passed several other people who were on the way down. They shouted at him, but chose not to pursue. Jiri was driven enough to ignore them. After reaching the fourth floor, Jiri stopped. The white corridor with the central runner that didn't sit straight caught his attention. The space buzzed with atmosphere. It rumbled with reverb and scattered whispers. Far down the hall, light illuminated the hallway as one of the apartment doors blew open by the force of Pavel Fleischaker. He strolled out, talking back into the apartment to a faraway voice.

"It is okay, it really is okay," Pavel reassured the unseen figure. "I'll go bother the neighbours. I'll see if they can shine some light. I'm sure they will have plenty to say."

Jiri pressed against the wall and tried his best not to be seen. When he realized Pavel wasn't looking his way, he walked steadily along the red-patterned carpet runner, stalking, getting closer as quietly as he could.

Pavel lit a cigarette – likely given to him by another happy-to-please officer in the apartment. The officer either had one to lose or just wanted to keep the peace.

Pavel walked away from Jiri, along the corridor until he came to an apartment door. He sniffed the odours around. Pavel wasted time and held his hand out to knock, dragging his breath through the glowing, smoke fuelled cigarette. Jiri hid behind a piano stool that had been left out in the corridor. Pavel did not care to look anywhere but forward as he reached out his hand once more and gave the neighbour's door three solid taps. While he waited for somebody to answer he puffed away at his cigarette that now dangled precariously from his lip. Jiri held back until the door opened, and a middle-aged woman in her gown answered, "Yes?"

"Detective Pavel, StB. You are aware that something has happened in the apartment behind me, I wonder if you have a few minutes to, sit, talk and share anything you might have heard, seen, or otherwise..." Pavel spoke in an almost civilized manner despite the cigarette clenched between his teeth.

As the woman answered, Jiri took this moment to make it all the way to the apartment door behind Pavel's back. This had to be where his father was working. Jiri turned to face the door, taking an outstretched hold of the doorknob as, from behind, Pavel reached into his pocket, within sight and range of Jiri. The sly boy froze, and thought only of being caught. Standing back to back with Jiri, still unaware of his proximity, Pavel took his writing pad out and walked into the lavender-infused apartment. The door closed and Jiri sighed in relief.

Jiri opened the apartment door away from Pavel, and expected to see his father working a simple crime scene – either dusting for prints or talking to a witness. Maybe it was a simple case of stolen goods or even just a lead from a case that had erupted elsewhere. Startled by the amount of light that streamed in from the open window, the sudden clatter and flash from a camera bulb disorientated him further. He looked around to see if his father was still there.

The room was filled with off-white Bergere furniture. There was furniture with harsh angular table legs, sweeping edges. Not a right angle in sight. Then there was brown stuff on the wall between the two windows. There was a great spray of red turning a rusted brown along the rug at the side of a sofa, which faced away to the window. The room smelt like tainted metal, bad body odours and was also damp with mould. Jiri could not see what was beyond that area, but was suddenly aware of the people in the room. A photographer snapped away at the side of the couch to something Jiri could not see. It was a head. It was a head with long hair, but it was matted in blood and lord knows what else. Jiri staggered back, taking a hold of the grand old armchair that sat behind him, bunched into a corner.

Life popped...

Everything stopped...

In that moment, Jiri saw another flash as the room suddenly went dark and silent, and all of a sudden, everything was dreamlike.

#

In the dream, the apartment door flew open and struck the grand old armchair in a similar manner that Jiri had done before. The door opened so hard that there was a chance it would unhinge itself from the wall.

Two people ran into a curtain-drawn darkened apartment. A woman wearing a white dress bounced excitedly into the nearby bedroom. A man followed behind her into the apartment, knocking the arm of the grand old wooden chair on his way in. He was not in such a hurry. He slammed the door shut and looked over at the chair. It was then that Jiri realized he was in the room with them. Jiri felt as though he wasn't really there. More so, it was as if he were staring at events through a thin veil. It was jarring, yet clear and tingling. The man who was now looking straight at him had no face. Any features, any strike of light had been covered by the brim of his hat and his high upturned collar on his coat, all of which obscured his face. He wore black gloves that reached out to Jiri's face. Jiri could smell the oiled leather from his glove.

"Jiri..." the man said. "Now I see you..."

Jiri was paralyzed.

Jiri's hands gripped the armchair as if they were bound to it. There was no letting go. The dream shimmered and flitted into sporadic waves of heat. The vision of the dark man loomed over him, and within moments, Jiri saw him lift his boot and then shunt it heavily against the chair, slamming it hard into the wall.

The grand old chair rested off-angle in the corner of the room as it was... as it had been before.

Jiri's vision blistered to darkness. Everything sped up. The man and the woman were in every part of the apartment like a morphed stretching substance like nothing he'd ever seen. He saw the violence, and he saw the blood as it hurtled across the floor and walls. The sound of a woman screaming filled his ears, followed by the whisper of a name that looped over and over in his mind.

Healy.

Tobe Healy.

4

U SMALTOVNY APARTMENT

MOMENTS AFTER

"Healy! Tobe Healy! Healy..." Jiri squirmed in the chair as a pair of hands tried to restrain him. As Jiri opened his eyes, the brightness of the room made him struggle some more. The concerned face of his father was paired with the realization that they were his familiar arms that held him down on the carpet of the apartment. That smell of rust and stench of organic mess forced Jiri to come about and regain his calm. There were StB officers standing around, all with serious faces and sorrowful expressions. Jiri looked up at the door and saw Pavel peering through the door, still smoking the nub of his cigarette. Pavel smirked behind his ugliness.

"Jiri, can you hear me?" his father said, as he

gave him one last shake-up to get his focus and attention. Jiri nodded, not taking his eyes off Pavel, who slinked away, smiling, back into the corridor.

"Look at me, Jiri." Nikolai demanded. Jiri turned to him, felt the chill of the room and saw the bloodstains on the walls and floor. He now knew how they got there. He knew more than anybody who stood around. The top of the woman's head was still against the couch arm. Sure enough, Jiri knew it was the woman from his dream. He heard the echo of her blood-curdling screams before passing out cold in his father's arms.

Nikolai carried his sleeping son, made his excuses to his comrades, and headed out into the corridor. Pavel followed him out.

"Are you taking the boy home?" Pavel asked.

"Yes, Pavel, he should not have seen any of this. It's my fault."

Pavel nodded as they reached the staircase. The cogs in his head were spinning with questions.

"How do you suppose he came up with that name?" Pavel asked and then exclaimed, "It was the chair this time, Nikolai. It was the chair!" Pavel stubbed his cigarette on the top step of the staircase and threw his hands up. Pavel stayed put on the fourth floor landing, and called down to Nikolai as he raced down the steps with Jiri in his arms.

"This is getting a bit too close for comfort if you ask me, Nikolai." Pavel yelled out for all to hear. He returned to the apartment and looked down at the armchair. He gave instructions, clearly.

"I want that chair sequestered."

#

Nikolai was angry with himself. During the car journey home he attempted to bury his feelings, even if Jiri did appear to be fast asleep on the back seat. He was however in two minds before it happened.

Sure Jiri should have been fine just sitting out in the car. Sure, he wouldn't get cold, or bored, or lack the human curiosity for his father's work that he had been kept away from

Nikolai knew that there was something of a pattern interrupt in the apartment that he couldn't put his finger on. Mr. Healy – or Tobe Healy as he would be named for now – always went in to connect the victim with the placement of the note. It would be a vase from the marketplace where he saw the victim for the first time. It would be a book that carried symbolism that would lead Nikolai to its discovery. For the hours he was in that apartment before Jiri's sudden arrival, Nikolai had been at a loss. The victim was completely random. The killing was just plain messy, too messy which meant, he had to have been distracted. The armchair was that distraction.

"But what if the chair was the opening? A conversation starter..." Nikolai's thoughts suddenly expressed themselves out loud. Jiri was therefore a distraction as well. Whatever Healy had planned, it all changed when Jiri turned up.

Jiri saw something. Mr. Tobe Healy had seen that "something" when he arrived at the apartment with the woman. It had been marked with the memory of the child who had put his energy out there no more than a day after the event.

Nikolai knew now that the now-named Tobe Healy had changed his game. He was now digging into Nikolai's inner circle. Any precognition that Nikolai had that day began and ended with picking up his son on his way to the crime scene. Nothing at the apartment stuck out, and it was as if Tobe Healy knew that Jiri was not only with Nikolai that day, but that he was going to be bored, cold, and curious.

This killer, Tobe Healy, was a force of nature with abilities that would be considered magic, mystical, rare, yet malevolent in the wrong hands.

Jiri touched the chair, and if only Nikolai had been aware that Jiri was sensitive to things like his mother was, then he would never have brought him along. Patricia, his wife, said that Jiri carried the sensitive gene, much like she had, but Nikolai denied that was true. Denial was a means of distancing Jiri from the possibility of a Tobe Healy being a part of his life as he was right there in his parents'. Nikolai and Patricia thought they had left Healy behind in Italy. Never thought for a moment that he would lie dormant and appear exactly where they had escaped. Prague was far, but never far enough. The very idea of: what you avoid gets bigger. What you don't deal with grows or follows you until it finds you. It cannot be ignored. It all applied to this very moment right now. Nikolai was kicking himself.

Unfortunately for Jiri, getting away from the crime scene would not be enough. Shamanic blood had been drawn, and the forces that he would follow the scent trail until he was found. Once Jiri is safe at home and awake, Nikolai will have to find out as much as he can about what he saw. Nikolai had to use this to their advantage. He had to put a stop to Healy's game soon, and with absolute finality.

Steps would have to be made to break the path. Once examined in a yet-to-be-determined undisclosed location, the grand chair from that apartment would have to be destroyed.

That was the link. That was the open door that Tobe Healy would reach through.

It had to have been a vision. Nikolai thought it through. He was the only one who could do the job of catching people like Mr. Healy... not that there was anybody like this to count, before or after. Who knew really? Mr. Healy had been around for a long time, and he wasn't about to be put to rest.

Not without a fight.

Tobe would usually leave messages on the body of his victims, especially if he wanted to say something private to Nikolai directly; nobody but Nikolai ever knew about it. Nikolai could arrive late on a case, the entire area having been swept through and cleaned out for evidence or anything linking to other crimes in the area. He would ask if there were any notes or messages.

"No, Nikolai," they said once, "you're wasting your time. This one has nothing to do with Mr. Healy."

Nikolai would walk around the room, pick up a book or an ornament, a vase, and straight away, either inside or underneath, he frequently found a little piece of paper that was fresh with Tobe's scrawl all over it. Although they were not signed, Nikolai knew who they were from. He knew it had to be him, and even though only until Jiri's encounter had a name been assigned to one of the most prolific killers since World War II, Jiri knew that Tobe Healy, by all accounts, was the man who had followed his family from Venice, Italy, to Prague. Of that there was no doubt.

When it became known that this serial killer was known from Nikolai's past – the secret police reacted very cautiously, taking him off cold cases and placing him on more regular routine assignments.

L'assassino di nota – or as he was known in English, The Note Killer, gave a reactionary response by murdering the pets of the other StB officers, gutting them and hanging them from a rope on their front door steps. Within a month, eight StB officers and several uniformed VB officers brought their cats, dogs, rabbits, and even a cockerel into the offices, all of which had a note tied to their blood-soaked legs with the message, in Tobe Healy's scrawl: Let N. Ivanov work.

The incident with Jiri also put the shoe on the other foot; so to speak, by putting L'assassino di nota back into Nikolai's inner family circle for the first time in over a decade.

Nikolai carried Jiri in his arms into the apartment and through the living room. There was subtle light coming through the heavy dark curtains of the living room, although to Jiri – who was half awake and half asleep – the daylight gave rise to images from the murder victim's apartment, flashing visions like sporadic sparks and pulses that he couldn't control. He felt his body being turned about as Nikolai carried him down the narrow corridor, past his mother's room, with its door ajar. They finally passed through into Jiri's bedroom, and the moment Jiri fell to his own bed, he exhaled. He turned his head, and squinted to see as his father headed out, leaving his door open to let in some light.

The living room suddenly burst into light as the sound of curtain hooks rattled across the rail, and brought in the full glare that reflected off the snow. He watched as his father headed down the corridor to Jiri's mother's room. Nikolai looked in, paused for a few moments, and then carefully closed the door before returning to the living room, where he stayed out of view for as long as Jiri could remain conscious.

5

THE IVANOV APARTMENT – 11PM

Jiri woke up to the sound of shuffling, breathing, and scraping. Each noise came and went without rhyme or rhythm. Although Jiri was awake now, he was vague about recent events. Because he was in his bed, he felt as though it could have easily been all a dream.

Gradually he tuned into what was happening in the apartment. Shuffle, scrape, inhale, exhale... shuffle. The sound was inside the apartment. Looking through the gap of his bedroom door, he saw his father's desk illuminated by an old oil lamp. The light brought the walls and the adjoining corridor to the front door to life. Wide-eyed, Jiri pieced together the source of the noise.

His mother's door was wide open, although the room itself was pitch-black. A dark shape emerged slowly from the opening. It was a box. The shuffle and the scrape was the noise the box made as it was inched slowly out of the room and into the dull light of the corridor. Jiri sighed in relief. It had nothing to do with that dream that he had. This was one of those everyday occurrences, and it was at least a good sign that his mother hadn't been wasting away in the room doing nothing. She had been creating things to sell for the market. She was making sure that the box was out ready for Jiri to take to the market on Saturday morning. Jiri sat up and watched as his mother's frail hands struggled to reach beyond her comfort of the darkness. The box began to scruff against the carpet runner which frustrated her even more. She needed the box to be in the middle of that corridor so that nobody would forget that it was there. Her fingers scraped in the inside of her room as she strained to reach and push the box into position. But the runner was still lifting, and it wasn't going to budge another inch. Jiri could hear his mother breathing more heavily. She was probably going to get angry with herself again if he didn't get out there and assist. Jiri still remained cautious as he left his bedroom. He tiptoed through the living room, noticing immediately that the curtains had been closed and that it was indeed the dead of night. His father was not home. The oil lamp he had lit was there to let Jiri know he wasn't going to be late.

But that didn't mean that he wouldn't ever be late. Jiri glanced at the clock on the mantle. It was eleven forty. He must have slept through…

Jiri suddenly flashed to something he didn't want to think about. He took in a deep breath, not wanting to deal with the sight of blood and rage. He needed to be strong now: strong for his Mother who was wailing and scratching at the side of the box with her long fingernails. Jiri approached the corridor.

'Mother?' he said softly.

Jiri watched as her hands continued to flail at the box in the attempt to give it one last push against the now gathered carpet runner. She wasn't about to emerge any further. She was already exposed and far beyond her comfort zone.

Jiri called out her name again, and this time, his mother's fingers grappled back from reaching and settled back into the darkness.

'Jiri?' she said with a soft croak as if she hadn't talked in weeks. Jiri listened as she struggled to gather herself on the ground. Jiri settled behind the box, now on his knees - just like his father had instructed when it came to communicating with her when she was sick. Jiri could see her outline: hair ends lit up haphazardly, all thick and wild and her eyes glistened in available light. She sighed, sunk inward and then spoke with the best motherly voice she could find.

'What day is it Jiri?'

Jiri thought for a moment before answering. It was close enough to midnight now. To say it was Thursday might confuse her further. 'It is Friday, early morning.'

'Ahh, good. I didn't miss the market. I promise I've been working. You can take this box to market for me tomorrow.'

Jiri nodded. He then held back a yawn. He didn't want to be told he had to sleep. He still wanted to find something to eat. He wondered if he should ask the same of his Mother, but his Father told him never to give her anything until he got home himself, even if she asked.

'I know I don't look myself right now, but once you see all the beautiful masks, the scarves and gloves I knitted, the carved animals especially will bring in the money.'

'I'm glad mother. I will take them to the market. Reznik will be there anyway, so you won't have to worry.'

There was a visible sign of a nod. He had worked the market in his mother's place several times already and had the glass maker, Reznik Killian follow her instructions to the letter.

Jiri wanted to say something else, but as they sat there, at stalemate, he did nothing else but smile. He let his eyes wonder to the box, and in that moment, the bedroom door slammed hard. It was as if a gust of wind had slapped him across the face. Jiri's heart skipped a beat. This was not out of the ordinary. Once she had had enough, she often disappeared back in a manner that always shocked him. He listened at the door for a moment, heard no voices. No wailing or crying this time, which meant she was likely, headed back to her bed for a well-earned sleep.

He carried the box away from her door. Out of sight, out of mind. He remembered what his father had said in the car when he had been caught playing truant. Other than that, everything else was a blur.

Jiri would not be going to school on this day: Friday, and was to remain at home until Monday, and for added bonus, he didn't have to go to gym class. Oh yes, he remembered that part.

Despite all the perks, he knew he wouldn't dare play truant again. Karel would have something to say about it when he passed by the market on Saturday. Jiri would embellish his punishment saying that he was struck down for his wrongdoing. He would have to let Karel know that it was never worth the fear.

Jiri's attention shifted to the subtle sound of whistling that came from the outer hallway. The bright and tuneful song from the British Isles: "Pop Goes the Weasel".

Jiri scuttled to the front door and spied through the peephole. At night, such a jovial tune coming from the lips of any man would mean one of two things: either he was heavily intoxicated or he was in love. Jiri knew that the whistling came from a neighbour, Mr. Dolya, who lived two doors down from their apartment. He had returned from being out, doing whatever men without family did.

Naturally, he gave out a whistle to let Jiri know – if he was awake – that he was back. The whistle also attracted the attention of another neighbour. Mrs. Roth could be heard yelling down the corridor in her native Romanian tongue. Mr. Dolya did not respond. He never did when she started yelling. Jiri always wondered what she was saying and would one day ask Mr. Dolya if he understood her raging barks or merely ignored them as the rest of the residents did. She was a shouter, and Jiri was always wary about making any noise when he passed her in the corridor or even in the street.

Mr. Dolya had been a reliable friend and neighbour of the Ivanov's ever since they arrived in that apartment building, and through thick and thin, he'd been there as a means of support for Nikolai – keeping an eye on Jiri whenever Patricia battled her demons.

Jiri headed out into the dark corridor, and saw Mr. Dolya's front door had been left ajar. Jiri peered into the apartment and saw Mr. Dolya who was in the process of lighting every the oil lamp that he owned; each one seemingly set an equal distance between one another. Jiri saw a food canister steaming over by the kitchen counter. The type that a mountain climber might take with them on hikes that lasted more than a day. Mr. Dolya turned and gave a kindly smile to Jiri.

'Jiri! I honestly didn't expect you here this late.' Mr. Dolya walked over to his window; his shallow severe cheeks were stretched with the smile that never went away. He pulled up the pane and allowed a white snowball cat inside. She curled her tail around his arm as he pulled the window down shut.

'It's too cold outside. Even for cats.' Mr. Dolya continued as Jiri -familiar with his surroundings - headed over to the kitchen, opened a cupboard door and retrieved his favourite bowl, as well as a plane white one for his friendly neighbour. Mr. Dolya was all over giving Snowball attention as she purred, now at his feet, curling that tail of hers lovingly between his ankles. Mr. Dolya pulled a tin out of the high open cupboards and closed the door. 'This little stray is new. I'm trying her with sardines tonight. If she likes them, I know I can get more.'

'She looks like a snowball.' Jiri said as he retrieved a spoon and made his way to set two places at the table.

'A good enough name. I only have three other cats staying with me now. Jones didn't come back, I'm afraid. I know you were fond of him. It seems when one goes, another turns up. A never ending cycle.'

Mr. Dolya spooned out and carefully separated the fish meat into a small dish. Jiri pulled out a chair, and Semolina, a shorthaired black cat, gave him a quizzing if not irritable look. Jiri left the cat well alone and moved his place over to the next chair at the table and checked to see if there was another cat asleep. No cat present, he pulled the chair out and sat down.

'Your Father explained what happened today, and that you'd slept through since Thursday morning. You must have had a fever or something.'

'I don't think so. I feel fine.' Jiri sat confused for a moment, still searching his mind for a memory beyond his sleeping state.

'Never the less, you must be famished. I took the liberty of filling this flask from the eatery around the corner. Jiri, have you ever eaten goulash?'

Jiri thought on it for a moment. 'No, I don't think so, sir.'

Mr. Dolya turned to the cupboard and dug in to look for Jiri's special bowl. It wasn't there.

'Wait, I thought...' He looked up at the table and saw it was already set. 'Magic.' Mr. Dolya smiled, and then said cheerfully, 'you didn't have to set the table Jiri. But, thank you.'

Mr. Dolya placed a plate of small bread rolls that had been fresh that morning. They were already hard to the touch, but he assured Jiri that goulash did incredible things to even the most hardened crust. He poured the thick stew into Jiri's bowl. Jiri saw that it was extremely hot and gave out a little blow to cool it down. The blow evolved into a whistle - and to that, Mr. Dolya tutted.

'You know you mustn't whistle inside a building, especially of that which you live. It's bad luck.'

Jiri frowned, 'you whistle all the time Mr. Dolya. Why can't I?'

Mr. Dolya laughed, 'I do it when I pass Mrs. Roth's apartment. She's a bit of a cat manipulator. She was feeding Semolina old milk in the hallway. Poor thing got sick. She even tried to put on a string collar with the name of Dráteník. I had a feeling Mrs. Roth was superstitious.' He paused and then leant in as if ready to share a secret. 'Did you know, whistling is bad luck if you do it inside a building? It's like a curse, a hex that is said to set into motion, ghastly events. I myself don't believe any such nonsense. It doesn't make sense. Whistling does nothing to affect wood, the floors, the ceilings, or anything else for that matter, nor can a sound be the cause of a person's misfortunes. It seems the superstition extends only to those who whistle inside but how does a nature, any nature distinguish what is inside and what is outside. So I will carry on regardless.'

Jiri thought again, still a little confused. 'But you told me not to whistle? Why?'

'Good question.' Mr. Dolya thought for a moment. 'I don't know what your parents believe. The summoning whistle is a very common superstition. Some might even say: a curse. I'm sure your father is a man of great intelligence but even he, or even your mother, could have a weakness for superstitious beliefs. I wouldn't want to get you into any more trouble.'

More trouble? Jiri thought. He wondered what

he was meaning by that. There were times when he might have struggled with things and shown his frustrations, but that was common for any child. Even Jiri – a great observer of his peers – knew that. Oh, but there was running away from school, with Karel the other morning. Perhaps Mr. Dolya meant that. I'm sure Father would have told him about that.

'You think whistling inside is bad here.' Mr. Dolya mused between mouthfuls. 'In Thailand (formerly Siam), it is believed that if you whistle after dark there, then you would be in serious trouble. You see, the people believe very strongly that whistling after dark summons very unpleasant spirits and unrelenting demons.'

Jiri felt the hairs spring up across his neck, like a brush of wind or a vibration that made the bones behind his ears ache and throb. He suddenly flashed a memory - something about curtains and a blood-soaked rug, and a man in a raincoat with a solid boot. Thump!

'Eat your goulash.' Mr. Dolya said as an unexpected footnote to his anecdote. Jiri pondered his own nightmarish memories.

'Did you ever get caught doing anything bad when you were young?' Jiri asked.

Mr. Dolya lapped up his goulash and waited a few moments. He was deep in thought.

'Did you have anything in mind, Jiri?'

'I didn't go to school this morning. I sort of, skipped it…' Jiri said as he played with his food.

'I know, but that was yesterday morning.' Mr. Dolya corrected. 'You've been in a sleeping stupor for longer than a day.'

Jiri felt suddenly heavy-hearted. He placed his spoon clunkily on the edge of the plate. He heard the cats - Snowball and Semolina - both scrapping over the last bites of fish.

Jiri suddenly heard the sound of a woman screaming.

'Mother!' Jiri gasped, but Mr. Dolya looked up from his plate, all calm and not at all concerned. Jiri clunked his spoon on the bowl's edge and excused himself from the table. 'I'm sorry Mr. Dolya. It's my mother, screaming again. I have to go.'

Jiri started towards the door before Mr. Dolya was even able to call after him. Instead, he muttered under his breath in Jiri's absence.

'I didn't hear anything.'

Jiri hurried across the hall, pulled out his key from his pocket and fumbled with the lock. He rattled the lock. Never in his twelve years had he felt his heart so high in his throat ... not since.

Not since the apartment. The blood and Tobe Healy's boot!

He opened the door, ran straight in, and nearly tripped over the box that was left packed and ready on the carpet runner. He heard a soft murmur from behind his mother's bedroom door. He reached for the knob but pulled away against his better judgement. He had never opened her door when she was sick without his father being there. She had screamed before, for sure, but he had sat vigil against the door and sang her to what he hoped was an almost peaceful sleep.

This was different. No song was about to come from Jiri's mouth. He needed to look in. He needed to see her for sure. He reached once more for the knob.

'Jiri. I wouldn't do that.' Mr. Dolya whispered as he lifted Jiri's arm away from the door. 'You really shouldn't be alone with her. Wait until your father comes home. If she's quiet, then she is resting.'

'But... she just screamed.' Jiri panted. 'I should go and check to see if...'

'I didn't hear anything, Jiri. You probably heard the cats fight outside, that's all. Nothing else.'

Jiri blew the wind out of his cheeks. He thought for a moment and realised Mr. Dolya was probably right.

Jiri was still shaken when he sat back down at the table in Mr. Dolya's apartment. He looked at his goulash and felt sick at the thought of taking another mouthful. Mr. Dolya let Semolina out of the window. She scampered across the fire escape and along the window ledge. They were four floors up, and no matter what the drop, those cats found their way around, down and up again with an exacting skill. City cats were made of the tough stuff. It was then that Jiri realised that he had to be just like the cats.

Toughen up. Be a man. Jiri took his spoon and in spite of himself started to eat the now-cooled stew. Mr. Dolya was right about one thing. He was famished.

'This doesn't seem like a cold, or a fever.' Mr. Dolya noted as he sat back down at the other side of the table. He struck a match to light a cigarette. 'Something happened to you, didn't it?'

Jiri nodded. 'Yes, but I don't remember.'

'Try. Let's go back. You ran out from school with your friend. Cold morning…'

'It was foggy too.' Jiri added.

'Cold and foggy. Your father caught you.'

'Yes. Did my father tell you that?'

'Let's just say that he asked me to make sure you had a decent meal, and to look out for a young man by the name of Karel, should he come by the apartment. As far as your mother is concerned, giving her space at this time of night is probably a good idea, at least until your father comes home.'

Jiri tried hard to see through the fog in his memory. He had never lost a day before in his life – of which he could recall anyhow. This was strange for sure. He didn't feel at all like his usual self.

'Father told me to wait in the car. That's what I did. I waited inside the car.' Jiri suddenly remembered something. 'He left the car and went inside the building to work. I'm not allowed to see him work… usually, but he didn't want to leave me at home. Maybe because I was sick... like he said. I was under blankets, but I got cold, and bored.'

'Hmm.' Mr. Dolya made a noise and flicked his cigarette ashes into his empty bowl. 'Was that when you went inside the building after your father?'

Jiri knew the answer to that but didn't want to say. He did go inside, all the way up to the fourth floor to the place where his father was working. But...

There was more.

There was a lot more to it and as Jiri remembered, tears began to roll down his cheeks.

Mr. Dolya looked across without emotion. He knew that whatever the boy had seen was tied to being right in the middle of a case that his father was working on. Nikolai couldn't talk about it, and everything that was known was only the whispers of dramatic hearsay: Tall tales, fabrications, and exaggerations of actual events were the sum of it. Mr. Dolya revelled in the opportunity to get something from Jiri that nobody would ever know - exclusive knowledge, about any crime, happening right now in the city.

But still, Mr. Dolya had to tread carefully.

'I'm sorry, Jiri. You are probably still traumatised about what you saw inside.'

'Yes.' Jiri said staring across the room into nothingness.

'What did you see, Jiri?' Mr. Dolya asked.

'A chair. A wooden chair.'

'Go on... what else?' Mr. Dolya pushed.

'A man and a woman... and blood. A lot of blood.'

'Go on...' Mr. Dolya's eyes widened. He leant forward, but in that moment the door swung open from behind. Mr. Dolya turned to see Nikolai Ivanov, as timely as ever, standing somewhat pensively against the frame.

'Jiri.' Nikolai said softly. 'It is good to see you're up and about.'

Mr. Dolya immediately adjusted his pose. He stubbed out his cigarette end onto his plate and stood to attention.

'Nikolai!'

Jiri's father nodded. Jiri smiled at his father and then turned to Mr. Dolya 'Do you mind if I get down from the table?'

Mr. Dolya nodded, and Jiri hopped down and ran to his father for an embrace.

'Has he been good?' Nikolai asked Mr. Dolya.

'Always. He seems to have recovered well. He still needs to eat more.'

'Of course.' Nikolai leant down to Jiri, asked him to thank Mr. Dolya, and to go wait in the apartment for him. Jiri did so and left Nikolai and Mr. Dolya to talk.

Like adults did from time to time.

Even though Jiri was told to go straight home, he felt compelled to wait in the corridor for a lingering moment, and eavesdrop on what his father had to say to Mr. Dolya. It was likely going to concern him anyhow. Jiri felt something, a strange air of awkwardness between the two of them. He listened.

'What were you asking him about before?' Nikolai asked.

'The boy didn't know how he got home, that's all. I was trying to help him remember.'

'He just has a fever, that's all.' Nikolai said.

'I was concerned. He seemed traumatised. Said he saw blood. A man and a woman...and something about a chair.'

'He's probably had a few bad dreams, that's all. I thank you again for taking the trouble to look after him.'

Mr. Dolya paused before answering. He looked Nikolai in the eye and it was as if they both knew Jiri had not had nightmares. Nikolai couldn't cover it any more than that. Either he accepted it or not - it would have to do.

'It was my pleasure as always.'

Jiri listened no more. It seemed the pleasantries were already ending the conversation. Nikolai said goodnight and headed towards the door. Jiri ran inside and waited for his father to enter.

Nikolai arrived and stepped over the box that sat close to the front door. He checked Patricia's door and then headed to Jiri who had found a comfortable spot on his father's grand bureau chair.

Nikolai touched Jiri's forehead and then checked his pulse on his neck. 'Are you feeling better?'

Nikolai knew Jiri's head was still filled with

images of that apartment where the murder took place. Telling Mr. Dolya so much already was something that was bound to happen sooner rather than later.

Nikolai looked across at the bureau top and noted something out of place. It was a bowl and a spoon, but not one from their cupboard. At first he dismissed it, but then he recalled that Jiri had left a half-eaten bowl of goulash on Mr. Dolya's table.

'Does that belong to Mr. Dolya?'

Jiri stared over at the bowl and gasped.

'What's that doing way over here?' Jiri asked.

'I don't know. Did you bring it over from Mr. Dolya's apartment?'

Jiri thought for a moment, and then shrugged.

He did not remember. He knew he'd gotten caught playing truant with Karel. He recalled sitting in the car, out in the cold waiting for his father to return, and then waking in the apartment the first time and seeing his mother push the box across the corridor. He also remembered that he'd not been well, but what he didn't know if it was he who had taken the bowl off the table, and carried it back with him. He'd never done that before so it certainly wasn't a regular habit.

Jiri knew there was something wrong, but didn't understand what had taken over his mind.

'Father, what's wrong with me?'

Nikolai held him tight in his arms.

'Nothing, my son. Nothing at all!'

As he was led back to his bedroom with his

father's help once again, he climbed into his bed and hoped that he would remember how he got there when he woke up, hopefully the next morning, things could start afresh.

It was Saturday after all. There was no school, and market day would be a great distraction.

He had that, at least, to look forward to.

6

PRAGUE, CZECHOSLOVAKIA

SPRING – 1942

Patricia was allowed to survive the war, somehow.

Some attributed it to Nikolai's protection over her. He had rich connections and respect amongst Czech police force that remained strong even when they were overshadowed by the German occupation. Others attributed it to the support given by market seller Reznik Killian and his glassware stall on the market square. Most of the time, Patricia remained hidden in the apartment: working, stitching, fixing, hemming, and other garment-related repairs. That was her skill, and during wartime when things were tight, usefulness was always vital. Once the day's work of fixing and fabrication, she would move to more personal, creative pursuits that harked back to her days supplying handmade crafts to gift shops at her old haunts within the Jewish quarter of Venice.

The German invasion had forced Patricia to put away daily habits and religious restrictions. It was as if they were stored in a keepsake box in a deep winter wardrobe, hidden behind boots and fur coats. Christmas was celebrated as the accepted tradition. She learnt to sing the songs in German, but thought about them in Hebrew. Both worlds were kept separate. She even dyed her hair blonde and wore appropriately smart Western attire, both in public and in private.

Her fluency in German was - as it had to be - clear and precise; even the Germanic colloquialisms she collected were used in her natural way of speaking. Once a week, on a Saturday evening, as she bathed, she whispered in Hebrew a request to be pardoned for her transgressions. Every morning as she washed at the basin, she would pray and repent with the promise of giving to charity to ensure that God saw her as being faithful despite their community of silence. She prayed that all of this fear would end.

To combat her depression, at times Nikolai would bring her gifts that were either Venetian in origin or a reminder of the life before her part-captive lifestyle; be they books, postcards, clothing or even flowers. She always longed for flowers no matter what the season.

It was her love of flowers that opened the door to a lasting friendship with Reznik Killian. Nikolai had purchased an authentic Venetian vase from Reznik's store in the spring of 1942. On this occasion, Nikolai also bought her favourite springtime bloom, the Siberian Wallflower. Patricia was thrilled and displayed them on his desk so they could both enjoy them together. She then noticed, looking close up at the base of the vase, holding it up to the lamp that the markings, the thickness of the stem and overall clarity of the sand appeared rushed. She determined after a few moments that it was not Venetian.

'Are you certain?' Nikolai asked when presented with the suspicious vase. 'The seller was very adamant that he got his shipment from a well-known Burano glassmaker.'

'Burano? Didn't he mean Murano? Burano is known for its lace, not its glass.' Patricia said with a raised eyebrow that screamed: I'm right, and I know it.

'Nikolai, this man is selling fake Venetian goods.'

Although disappointed, both Patricia and Nikolai realised that this discovery of counterfeit goods was at least a distraction from the monotony of the severity of day-to-day life. It however was not a life and death ordeal. Civilians handled things on the level, as equals before matters were ever escalated to the police. In wartime, it was the unwritten rule of survival: Don't throw your peers overboard for the sharks.

'I'm curious about what else he is selling.' Patricia added. 'Can I go with you to the stall?'

'Should we take back the vase?' Nikolai answered first.

'Was the seller German?' Patricia asked. That presented a complication: You dare not foil the ruling establishment. You never know how deep their connections.

'I don't think so.' Nikolai thought a little more. 'He didn't seem like an immigrant either. I'd hate to say it, but he's probably one of those former factory owners from the west who had their buildings seized by the Germans. I've heard of people like him that hung onto their trade-skills. A man like that doesn't just come out of nowhere. These are after all hard times, and he's probably trying his utmost to cover his losses.'

Patricia sighed. She suddenly had a change of heart.

'Well in that case, let's keep it. It's a positive memory like any other. I'm sure he's selling them this way to make a little more money. He probably has a family to feed.'

It was amazing to Nikolai that although his policing practices would usually result in putting this man out of business for fraud, he would in this case have to be lenient. While the Germans had their boot-hold in the city, there was a shift in the measurement of crimes and misdemeanours. These were offences that were big enough to take action, but when many struggled to get through with their heads held high, the community turned a blind eye to such minor discretions. It was necessary or the whole community would be outing each other for personal gain rather than justice.

Patricia's eyes lit up. She had a thought. 'Perhaps we have an opportunity here.' She said. 'After all, wouldn't the Venetian glassmaker stall look better if he had authentic Venetian items to sell?'

'Yes.' Nikolai said with a great smile. 'Very much, yes!'

Nikolai might have had something to do with Patricia's survival during the war, but it was moments like this that made him realise that she could've done well enough without any help. He agreed to the outing. It would be a very rare daylight venture for Patricia. They would both head out when the Wednesday trade set up shop in the early hours of the morning.

Very early hours of the morning...

'We can get some blue scorpion grass to contrast the orange wallflowers.' Patricia said with a smile. Nikolai returned the smile. He wanted her to be happy, no matter what. She was aware of the dangers, but sometimes, risks in life were necessary for positive things to happen.

That Friday night, as always, Patricia and Nikolai fell asleep together in each other's arms. However, by 2am, Patricia awoke from a nightmare. Her hands shook as she gripped the sheets. Nikolai bolted upright and placed a supportive hand on her shoulder.

'What is it?' Nikolai asked, still foggy from the sudden alarm. She then screamed out, thrashed her hands above her as if fighting away the night demons that haunted her dreams. Once she calmed down, she found her words.

'I can't go tomorrow. They'll see me, and they'll see through me and know that I don't belong. I don't deserve to be here, and I can't risk losing you. I won't go to the market with you!'

'That's okay... You don't have to. I can visit the stallholder myself. I promise I will get that proposal across. He'll go for it. I'm certain of that. You don't have to worry.'

Patricia nodded and acknowledged that it was most definitely the right decision to stay behind. She was glad that common sense came to her before making a big mistake. It wasn't worth it. Even with the possibility of opportunity, it wasn't worth it.

She lay on her back and stared at the ceiling. Nikolai turned away and soon began to drift back to sleep. Patricia's eyes stayed open. No less than ten minutes later, Patricia nodded after giving her thoughts a good run for their money. She turned back to Nikolai and whispered in his ear.

'I can't hide forever. I will go tomorrow. I will wear a disguise if I have to.'

Nikolai opened his eyes. To him, she sounded calm and had obviously given this a lot of thought. He turned his head and looked at her face. Nothing needed to be said, but nonetheless, he nodded and then put his thoughts across gently.

'It's up to you.' Nikolai whispered back. 'But you're with me. I won't ever let anything happen to you. Not again.'

WEDNESDAY MORNING, 5:45AM

Patricia patted down her body with pale powder, put on make-up, adorned herself with her blonde Scandinavian woven wig, and put on her elegant and elitist long overcoat. To finish off, she slipped on her sheepskin gloves and Austrian-made shoes to ensure the greatest distraction from her face. They clunked loudly, announcing her arrival. The footwear may have been a brash choice, but that was how, in her mind, she had fought her war against the Germans.

Distraction.

#

The sun scraped its way over the red rooftops of Prague. The morning was busy with the abrupt noise of soldiers moving about town with big hangovers and very little grace and care. This was something the locals would never get used to. The Prague natives kept quiet, even in the market stalls where having a voice to sell was deemed vital; such business was exercised in hushed tones and eyebrow gestures while the German officers looked over them. There were rare moments of gunfire, usually from outer regions of Prague, where the resistance filtered through, constantly moving, racing to the countryside in times of desperation. Homeless families were immediately forced by troopers to move. Any questions concerning their rights to live were treated with immediate hostility.

Patricia had seen very little opposition during her afflicted confinement. Her shock at seeing the world around her being pulled inside out, as it were, was almost too much to handle. Today however, she was compelled. She pushed herself because of a feeling, and with that, she held her head high as she left the apartment block and walked with Nikolai hand-in-hand through the residential blocks and over the crossroads towards the city's main high street.

There were two bodies on the main road that morning, both covered with potato sacks, waiting and rotting until somebody claimed them. Many so-called witnesses said this was an accident, but Nikolai could read the situation. There was a wagon that had been stripped down and left at the side of the road. A lot more blood was spilled separate from the two covered bodies. Patricia whispered into Nikolai's ear about an overwhelming feeling of suffering.

'A horse was shot here.' She told him as she read the situation. 'It wasn't even an accident or even some kind of mercy killing. They drilled that poor animal with bullets.'

She stopped for a moment and scanned the entire street. There was more to it than just empathic sensations. She could hear and even smell the tragedy as it happened over and over. Although she didn't say anything to the fact, Nikolai knew that the scene before them was truly loaded.

Nikolai read the clues and explained that the wagon stopped here was most likely full of inappropriate contraband. The Germans seized the contraband and killed the horse and two riders. The horse was likely taken away from the crime scene by a desperate civilian and likely sold good and fast to a butcher for ready cash.

'Once they remove the bullets, all that tainted meat will be stripped and put out for quick sale.' Nikolai said. 'Nobody will dare ask where they got it from.'

They walked on a little further until Patricia noticed something as they passed a side street. She saw something else: an older German officer held a crying baby. There was a wooden dreidel lying amongst the possessions that lay scattered on the ground. Bloodstains dripped along the sloping edge of a window ledge. She tracked her eyes to the ground where she saw the face-down bodies of two adults, dead and partially covered, out of sight and out of heart.

'Another family that just couldn't get away fast enough. Such haste and carelessness, getting caught so easily...' Patricia choked on her words. She grabbed a hold of Nikolai's hand. They walked on from the scene until there was nothing more to see. Within moments, they emerged onto the edge of the market square, smiling, holding hands, just like any regular couple heading to market day. 'Don't ask me what they did with the baby.' She finished. Her eyes glazed and she trembled slightly with a sudden intake of breath. Nikolai nodded. He didn't need to ask. That child was not likely to be alive by sunset.

Queues had already started to stretch from the doors of the courthouse, wrapping along the gates and spilling out onto the main street. The train station was packed with workers and "chancers". The walls and even the windows were covered with large pictorials depicting a heroic Adolf Hitler surrounded by the children that represented the future of Germany after the war was won.

Finally, the market loomed and a sense of comfort came along with it. Various stallholders shook off their dew-covered awnings and wiped down the benches that allowed their patrons to stay longer. They allowed any German soldier first pickings, even before they were out on display - from the perishable and more exotic purchases. They were obviously given discounts that translated pretty much as, "what I give is what I pay!" promotions.

They witnessed the first conflict of the day: an argument between a seller of candles and a German officer who wanted too many boxes for a less than attractive profit.

'I have to save at least one box of the Roman candles for the parishioner; he has these on reserve.' Patricia heard as the argument passed their attention. Passive trouble was always better than being in the firing line of active dispute. It was not going to be a good day for that vendor, she thought. She tugged on Nikolai's jacket and informed him that they also needed candles.

'We should come back after the soldiers have moved on.' Patricia noted softly.

They turned the corner, past the fountain where a seller of meats and variety cuts was being called out by one of the resident butchers.

'Your meat is too close to mine! Why can't you be on the other end of town?'

'You better keep your voice down' the stallholder said, calling for calm, 'I've been given this spot now!'

Patricia watched as the row calmed down to intimate hushed tones. Neither stallholder wanted to be seen arguing.

Nikolai muttered into Patricia's ear. 'The stallholder and the city butcher will both give in, don't you worry. You'll see when the crowds come;

they will end up endorsing each other in good spirits.'

Patricia smiled and replied, 'I still need to buy your lamb for tonight. Which one should we go to?'

'Neither. There's a new butcher at the far end, close to the glass merchant. He comes secretly kosher guaranteed.'

Patricia shushed and smiled at the same time. It was risky to say the word kosher in public, but Nikolai was cockier than most.

'Oh! Is that where you've been getting our meat? You never told me it was... it was... blessed.'

'I don't always kiss and tell.' Nikolai pointed, changing the subject. 'There's your glassmaker.'

Patricia looked over at a stall which was partially set up with all things she had associated with her upbringing in Venice: there were vases, tall and small, all marked with the distinction of being authentic Murano glass. There were bottle stoppers, glass figurines of dancers, animals, beautifully crafted, and yet - upon close examination of the pieces – Patricia could see repetitive flaws that had been "designed" to emulate the quirks of homemade glassware. Unless her homeland had altered its methods over the last few years of factory production - which was possible due to wartime constraints - then doubt would overcast near enough anybody's ability to judge.

She looked over at the trader himself for more

information: Reznik was a portly man whose head was larger than life. His hands didn't look like a craftsman's hands; they were somewhat clumsy looking. Patricia looked at him and questioned how he was able to craft anything that he sold. The vases, she understood, could be his work but the glass wine stoppers, the dancing, delicate figurines of elegance... they had to have been made by the very best glass workers Prague had to offer. The way that the glass was packaged was surely not a condition from which authentic glass from Murano would be packed if they were to survive the journey across on land freight, be it by train or otherwise.

'Good morning.' Nikolai spoke, keeping Patricia at his side as his silent partner.

'Ahh,' said Reznik, 'I remember you came to my store yesterday. I trust you are enjoying your wine stoppers?'

'He bought a vase from you in actual fact...' Patricia corrected with a raised eyebrow. Reznik gestured apologetically for forgetting such minor details. He didn't care about past purchases any more than he enjoyed small talk.

'My husband and I were wondering where they were made?' she asked, going straight to the heart of the matter.

The question left Reznik dumbstruck for a moment. He then laughed and connected the dots and making it look like he knew what he was talking about all along.

'Why Italy, of course! The shores of Venice hold many mysteries.' He pointed to the dancing sculptures. 'In Venice, the dancers, they dance all night to the pretty melodies of pipes. The taste of love is always in the air. Everything is at a good price. You won't see anything like this in all of Prague.'

Patricia furrowed her brow. 'I don't mean to be rude, but I've lived and worked in Venice, sir, as an apprentice to an established glassmaker--'

Patricia's words were drowned out by the sound of claxons. Two German UAZ off-road vehicles encroached along the market stall walkway, knocking over a carton of oranges in their tracks, much to the silent defeat of the stall owner, who stood aghast as the second vehicle rode over his oranges as they rolled along the cobbled streets.

The moment passed. Reznik appeared unimpressed by the commotion and called for the attention of his two patrons.

'You are a policeman, no?' Reznik asked.

'I am.' Nikolai said as he turned back to Reznik. 'But I'm here as a civilian. My wife and I have a proposition for you. We believe that your vases are not made in Venice at all. We might not be the only ones to notice this, and it would be good for you to perhaps include authentic Venetian craft and gift items to mix in; to further augment the vases and the glass figurines with the authenticity you can truly guarantee.'

Reznik stood silent. He digested what was said

and then gave the couple before him a smirk of amusement.

'I don't think your proposal is necessary. How can you get authentic Venetian "anything" around here?'

'I have skills. I can show you.' Patricia said sincerely with a nod of encouragement. Reznik puffed out the strain of air from his lips and crossed his arms with an air of defiance.

'I don't need anything from you. You could be Michelangelo or da Vinci himself, it would still be too dangerous. You know what I'm talking about.' Reznik said.

Patricia whispered into Nikolai's ear - a request to step away. She then said aloud, 'I'll walk to the flower stall. I want to get those forget-me-nots while they are fresh.'

Nikolai nodded and watched her walk away with a solemn smile. Nikolai turned to Reznik.

'Listen. I might not know you as well as you think you know me, but I have a feeling you come from a strong business background. You were doing pretty well for yourself before the war. You probably have a family to support. My wife is a skilled craftswoman. She merely wants to work, to keep life moving forward. We will happily cut you in for fifty percent of the profits if you give her a space in your stall.'

'Profits? What does she have to offer that I don't already have?'

'Authentic Venetian masks, dolls, hats, toys,

gifts, key chains.' Nikolai hushed his tone, 'Now you can play hard with me, but I can also play hard with you, sir. I take it this stall is your only livelihood? I would best reconsider ever speaking of your assumptions of "who is a Jew and who isn't", because whatever you do to us will come back to you tenfold. That's the way this world goes. Life around here is hard enough. None of us can afford to turn our back on opportunity. You have a life to pay for... this offer could provide your goods with a legitimate staple of Venetian authenticity. Nothing that you sell will be diminished. This is an offer to enhance and increase your profits. How can you say no to that?'

'Are you saying she's going to make all the vases too?'

'No.' Nikolai backed away as he saw two German troopers walking past with a green shirt soldier, whom they had brought with them to explore the city streets and keep the order. Nikolai noticed that the green shirt soldier was holding his uniform wrapped up in a bundle. He seemed in awe of the place, as if experiencing it for the first time. Nikolai and Reznik both waited until the three Germans passed before speaking in softer tones.

'You carry on; make your vases as they are.' Nikolai continued. 'This is not a time for picking apart personalities for doing whatever they can to get through the day, but surround your livelihood with authenticity and there can be no question. You will stand as a legitimate seller of Venetian wares.'

'This sounds too much of a good thing.' Reznik said with a furrowed brow. 'What's the catch? Who do you really work for?'

Nikolai gave out a great sigh and stared at the cobbled street at his feet for a moment before rising back to meet Reznik eye-to-eye.

'I'm Nikolai Ivanov. My wife is Patricia. You know where to find us. My wife is waiting for me at the flower stall. She has what she wants. They will still look great in the vase I bought from you the other day. Thank you good sir.'

Nikolai began to walk away. Reznik held off for several breaths before calling him back.

'I want to invite you to eat with us, this lunchtime; perhaps we can discuss it. How about the Pes a Kačica tavern in the west quarter? It's kosher. So I heard.' Nikolai returned with warmth in his eyes. He extended his hand.

'Please, sir, what is your name again?'

'Reznik.' He shook Nikolai's hand, strong and firm. 'Reznik Killian.'

#

As Nikolai and Patricia walked away with flowers and a paper-wrapped bag of lamb chops, they noticed a group of German foot soldiers who had gathered at the far side of the market strip. One of the young soldiers held what appeared to be a rolled-up grey uniform. He broke away with something of a sprint, and ran straight up to Nikolai and Patricia. They stayed calm. This German soldier was very wet behind the ears and came with more enthusiasm than any sense of menace.

'Excuse me, Mr. Ivanov.' The young German officer said, 'May I speak with your wife a moment?'

Nikolai hesitated for a moment feeling Patricia grip his hand tightly behind his back. He quickly reasoned with himself and nodded consent. The young German officer turned to address Patricia.

'Mrs. Ivanov. I have been issued a replacement uniform. You are known as the one to go to for stitching and needlework. I ask if you would do this.'

The request was polite. The two German officers behind laughed at the nervousness of the nugget foot-soldier.

Patricia was on show and proceeded as if he was as dangerous as any other German soldier. She nodded and spoke in her trained Bavarian tongue.

'Yes. I can do this for you. Please give me until the afternoon. You can pick it up at this address. A short walk from here.'

She quickly pulled out a piece of paper, and scrawled her address, complete with the German sharp s. She then handed it to the young soldier. He in turn handed her the trooper uniform in a bundle.

'My Panzer collar insignia has not yet been sown

onto the jacket. I trust you know where these go.'

Patricia nodded as she looked at the two slightly frayed pieces of dark grey material.

The young soldier suddenly remembered something else, and took out from his pocket another patch.

'I almost forgot this.' He gave the last patch to Patricia. She looked down at it for a while until her attention snapped back to the young soldier as he struck a strong gallant pose, arm extended outward.

'Sieg Heil!' He said as a part of his doctrine. Patricia and Nikolai both stood to attention, and with hidden reluctance and a sense of horror in their hearts, they returned the salute, and spoke the words, Sieg Heil, in return.

The soldier walked back to his fellow troopers and they went on their loud and merry way. The troubling sensations passed and yet Patricia and Nikolai stood silent for a moment. Patricia looked down at the last embroidered patch that she didn't care to name or even acknowledge. It went without saying that with every swastika she stitched onto every freshman's jacket that a little piece of her was ripped from its threads. She hated the thought that it was this job that she did well that kept her alive. But at least she would not be wearing it. If she didn't stitch the patch, somebody else would.

#

That evening, Nikolai watched in silence as Patricia sat on the floor, lit purely by candlelight. She carefully and delicately stitched the swastika onto the red wrap that would be pinned to the elbow of the uniform. She did so with a complete detachment. He looked across at the vase where the orange and blue flowers complimented each other. The flowers needed light.

They weren't the only ones.

7

PRAGUE, CZECHOSLOVAKIA

WINTER 1952 – SATURDAY – MARKET DAY

Jiri walked to the market with his mother's box of Venetian giftware neatly divided at the front and rear baskets of his bicycle. The snow had prevented him from actually cycling. No questions were raised for a boy who walked alongside his heavy load. It took him a full thirty minutes to get from the apartment to Reznik Killian's stall.

Jiri was glad to be out and about during the quiet mornings, for he had something of an anxiety for crowded places. As the hustle increased he would stay behind the tables and keep a safe distance. He was never the mingler, and always the watcher.

Prague as a city stood out like a museum to those times of fear and struggle. Relics of bomb-damaged buildings - many of which had been incorporated into the landscape – stood broken and lifeless, awaiting the rebuild that was long overdue. Many of the badly damaged been pulled down and gaps had been made. The first few years were about the resurgence of the economy and re-housing in areas where new housing could be built, fast and by the numbers. The priority was given to the historical monuments. All that made Prague a great city had to be saved.

Soviet tanks were still commonplace. They remained at station keeping alongside train lines and city limits. They became nothing short of window-dressing. The children saw things as they were without background or comparison.

This was their home.

This was how it was.

This was life.

It was the job of the uniformed VB officers to wander the streets in the early morning, and wake up the homeless from their sleep as they nestled under the bridges. In the winter, the constant smell of campfires created a dense smog about the city. The homeless were a mixture of war veterans and travellers, hermits and hospital patients who were way out of their territory, and had no choice but to wait in the streets until they healed enough to walk their way back home. They had no money to get anywhere beyond the overhang of the train station platforms.

This was how it was.

This was life.

A policeman with a wheelbarrow was not what Jiri expected to see appearing in the deep shadows of the side streets that morning. Jiri watched as he accompanied other policemen who proceeded to lift a heavy body from a vacant doorway. Covering their mouths, it was clear that they had yet another victim of the harsh winter cold – no doubt, this was a man who had been discharged from the hospital with no direction home.

The dead body was not what stopped Jiri in his tracks as he held onto the handlebars of his bike. It was what was left behind after the man's hasty removal from the doorway that kept him from moving on. Jiri saw that the vacant dwelling where the man had slept and died. It had an alluring glow to it. There seemed to be an imprint - a vague impression, as if the body of the man had never been taken away at all. It was nothing more than a ghost, a feeling, and despite Jiri's needs to push forward on his journey, something whispered to him. For some strange and indiscernible reason, he heard the name whisper delicately in the wind.

Healy...

Seeing Reznik's stall at the end of the market circuit gave Jiri a little comfort. Today, as it had been for as long as Jiri could remember, Reznik's stock of fake Venetian vases adorned the centre of his giftware stand. The rest of the stand was dedicated to his own crafting of wood and small glass figurines which had been confirmed to be all manufactured at his own home. Patricia had the corner table – the selling blind spot which during the war had been dedicated to gas masks, rubber boots and regulation socks all of which were now lost in the past. Patricia's items were at the very least complimentary to all. If anything, Patricia's work was eye-catching: the biggest seller being the Venetian masks (all different, with various motifs that explored music, love and the mystery of the masquerade.) She had educated Reznik about the fusing of glass to metal and also created the clear window boxes that contained his decorative fake bottle stoppers and fish knives. Patricia would also create Venetian rag dolls, hand fans, document wallets adorned with tassels. Regardless, Reznik was open to anything.

Jiri was always proud of the items that his mother made, even though he was never able to watch her as she crafted them. Patricia never liked onlookers and worked with the door closed, especially when she was sick.

Reznik opened Patricia's stock bundles and checked off on his own ledger each item, putting aside those that would be later added to snow globes or otherwise sold on privately to his own discretion.

'I need you to stay for an extra hour today.' Reznik seemed to explain what Jiri was doing without the need to really ask. Jiri nodded and placed the masks together in various display pots. Colour feathers jostled in the wind. The dead eyes of the masks stared back at him. The stoic angular mouths whispered words he could not quite understand. It was more of a rumble of tones, an uneven chant that cursed him through the air and then stopping everything around him.

Jiri's hands idly reached out to place another mask on a stick into the glass display pot. A glass candleholder in the shape of a swan brushed his elbow. It fell and shattered on the ground.

The sound caused a stir, and eyes all turned to Jiri's position. The harsh words of Reznik pierced the silence.

'What are you playing at? That swan just cost your mother four masks!' Reznik reached for a paper bag and a hand brush and passed it to Jiri. 'Now clean that up before somebody steps on it!'

Jiri felt shocked. Reznik had never really been this irritated with Jiri so early on in the day.

With brush and bag in hand, Jiri got down onto the cobbled street to clear up the mess. The glass was two tone: clear and orange comprised of one large piece surrounded by a scattering of little jewel pieces. Jiri touched the large piece and in that moment, his eyes went dark. A repeat image of impact rushed through his memory. He could see himself over and over, turning as he looked down at the swan as it hit the ground. The Venetian masks resounded and the sound of glass smashing against stone was both resonant and constant. It was as if he was experiencing the swan's demise over and over, from touch to impact, touch to impact.

Jiri pulled his hand away, and there suddenly he felt his skin break. He awoke as if emerging from another dark place; he pulled his hand back quickly and looked down at the cut on his hand. Blood lingered for a moment before slowly oozing and collecting through his skin.

Reznik rolled his eyes, 'I'm not going to have you bleed all over the floor. I'll clean this up; you go to the flower stall and get Evelyn to clean you up.'

Jiri was only half listening. His hearing competed with a slight ringing in his ears.

'Do you have any gauze or dressings, Reznik?' Evelyn asked.

'Not really.' Reznik sniffed. 'I expect people to be more careful.'

'I feel giddy.' Jiri said as he starred down at the sight of his own blood.

'Don't you dare faint on me boy!' She said gently. She looked back and Reznik. 'I'll bring him back to you in a moment Reznik, please, watch the flowers!'

Soon he felt Evelyn's hand pull his arm as he was escorted, dazed and confused, until he was settled on a chair inside a nearby tavern. The flower lady had wild flowing hair and always had a scent of fresh-cut flowers.

Reznik waved off his annoyance, shook his head

in preparedness for getting back to his daily routine.

Several moments later, Reznik had emptied Patricia's bundles, dusted down his own stool and sat for the remainder of the morning. Now that everything was out, Reznik didn't like to get up for anything; except profit. In the background, he heard a woman calling to him.

'Excuse me; are you in charge of this stall?'

Reznik turned to see an old lady holding a blue perennial plant and a small brown unlabelled packet of seeds. Reznik pointed towards a jar that he'd put at the end of the flower lady's counter top. He indicated to the patron to simply put the money into the stall holder's jar.

'Where is the flower lady today?' the patron asked.

'Oh she'll be back in a moment.' he said with impatient disinterest. 'Just put the money in her jar.'

'How do I know how much these things are?' the lady asked.

Turning again Reznik shrugged. 'Take a guess!'

The patron didn't say anything more, but Reznik heard the chink of change as it hit the bottom of a jar. The next sound Reznik heard was from directly in front of his own stall; the distinct crunching of glass. Reznik looked up to see a tall shadow of a man wearing a coat, a hat, a scarf that wrapped tightly around his neck. He wouldn't have thought he was even alive was it not for the outtake of breath that periodically drifted from the dark extremity that was, the man's assumed face. Reznik stood from his chair.

'My apologies for the glass. I thought I got it all.' Reznik announced. 'I hope it didn't pierce your boot.' Reznik then smiled a German Marks smile. 'What are you looking for today? A gift for a lady perhaps?'

The man in the long dark coat looked at the glass on the ground and decided to bend down to take a closer look. Reznik too moved under the stall to see what had caught the silent man's eye. He watched as the man slowly took off his glove and touched a piece of glass as it sat on the ground.

'Sir, I assure you the glass will be cleaned up. Perhaps you can just step to one side and we can talk--'

Just as Reznik's words trailed off, the man looked at him right in the eye. Still under the stall, looking across the darkness of the under-boards, Reznik was suddenly overwhelmed. He went to stand, but banged his head against the stall edge.

Reeling for a moment with the sudden bump, he cursed and then stood up to look the visitor above the boards. The man in the dark coat was already walking away. Nothing else needed to be said as Reznik rubbed the side of his head, cursing the man in silence. The knock caused his ears to ring ever so slightly. He watched as the man in the dark coat as he drifted off the market main walkway, into a side street, out of sight.

THIRTY MINUTES LATER

Evelyn, the flower stall woman, arrived back at the market front with Jiri whose finger had been cleaned and wrapped in vinegar-soaked gauze. To both their surprise, Reznik was nowhere to be seen.

Both Reznik's giftware and Evelyn's flower stall were unattended. Three customers waited with their flower choices with a mixture of concern and impatience.

'You go attend the glassware stall, Jiri. When he gets back from wherever he's gone, we'll give him hell for taking off.'

Jiri agreed and went to Reznik's seat. Remembering the glass, he set about clearing the fragments from the cobbled street. This time, he had the sense to grab a brush and some paper to scoop the now crunched and embedded glass from the market street. Once completed, he placed the folded paper with the glass under the stall with the brush laid atop. That was the best he could do right now. Jiri still felt uneasy. There was something strange about his day already.

He had no clue what Reznik was doing, or where Reznik had gone. Bathroom breaks, smoke breaks … whatever breaks he took, he was always in visual distance of his stand. He would never leave his livelihood unattended. He was a businessman. It just wasn't done. Jiri sat and waited allowing the worry to touch him with each passing thought.

MIDDAY

That afternoon, Evelyn corralled the attention of Mr. Dax Shandling, a very smart, somewhat debonair chairman of the marketing community. Jiri felt nervous. Dax Shandling was never spoken to unless something was extremely important. He would usually walk through and everybody would mind their own business. Evelyn spoke disparagingly about Reznik. Jiri had sat silent and listened. He had only put a few korunas in the pot while Reznik had been away. It was not going to make his mother happy. He didn't have the selling skills that Reznik had, and Jiri was sure he was letting the stall down by being there. He couldn't reason with himself that he was just looking after the goods, making sure they didn't wander. Street children walked by appearing tempted for a quick grab, but for some reason, they too eyed up the boy on the stall and thought better of it. Jiri might have been small, but had an air about him today. He had the feeling that something surrounded him. More hours passed and Jiri noticed Dax Shandling had returned after doing his rounds. This time, he headed straight to the glassware stall.

Straight over to Jiri.

'He hasn't come back, has he?' Mr. Shandling stated.

Jiri shook his head and leaned back a little to get out of the firing range of Dax's cigar breath.

'Mr. Killian can't just leave his stall open and unmanned. It goes against the agreement. I will have to take this all away and have it stored. He can pay a penalty fee for neglect.'

Jiri wanted to speak, but was afraid that he'd say the wrong thing. It was only now that he truly felt concern for Reznik's absence. He realised that his stock — a percentage of which was manufactured by his mother — was not going to go home with Reznik. Jiri knew also that he couldn't just box up his mother's goods and take them with him. Dax would surely think he was taking off with Reznik's business.

'I still can't believe Mr. Killian never told you where he was going?'

Jiri shook his head.

'Go home, Jiri Ivanov. I'll handle it from here.'

Jiri hung back by the flower stall and watched as Mr. Shandling and his subordinates hastily boxed up Reznik's stall. They were heavy-handed and did not care about how they wrapped — or half wrapped as Jiri saw — both Reznik's and Jiri's mother's fragile items. Jiri knew some of it would be damaged, and that would surely make Reznik blow his top.

Everybody was certain that Reznik was not going to return. It was a quarter to five, and ten hours without a stallholder present on a vitally busy Saturday must have been a serious issue. Jiri had a feeling, but didn't care to think about it. What was done was done, and it was Reznik's problem no matter how you looked at it.

'Go home!' Dax said, standing with arms crossed whilst leering down at Jiri who had remained on the stoop next to Evelyn's flower stall. Dax assumed a stance that Jiri couldn't argue with. He looked over for a reaction from Evelyn. She gave a grimace of disappointment and looked away. Jiri frowned at Dax and reluctantly, without any further question, he stood from the stoop and went on his way. He didn't ask about his mother's goods. Nobody would have listened to him anyway.

It was not right, that much was certain. But what could a kid like Jiri do?

Reznik shouldn't have left the stall. Jiri thought it through with empty questions. Why didn't he come back? Why can't I take Mother's things back to her ... why didn't I ask to take them back? He reached for his bicycle, feeling the essence of the dark voice that stood in the background of his mind. 'Is it my fault?' Jiri asked out loud to nobody but himself.

Yes ... Jiri heard a voice in his head that wasn't his own. Jiri ... it is all your fault!

It was only a feeling that was interrupted, when a woman in a full dress coat and a hat made a beeline to the packed-up glassware stall. Mr.

Shandling seemed surprised at first but then greeted the woman with warmth and consideration. The woman pointed to something and Shandling gestured that she be given what she came for.

The full box of his mother's Venetian items was passed to her and, she then pointed at other areas of the stall, and soon, other items were then gathered and placed inside the box. Jiri was confused for a few minutes. That was until he realised that it was his mother, out of her room and functioning as a human being once again.

This he did not expect, today at least. He still hung back and watched, knowing full well that being smothered or "surrounded" as it were, for such attention might tip the scale this early on in her return to grace.

It was always was like that.

Patricia was concealing her full appearance for she had come out of this darkness in a rush.

Jiri suddenly had a brainwave. His mother must have had one of her magic moments. She was here out of her fog at a moment when he needed her to be, and even though the thought never crossed his conscious mind, it was as if he'd summoned her out to be present.

How did she know? How did she know to come down? Jiri kept his thoughts to himself, but would share it with Nikolai later when he returned from his work for the day.

Or night.

Nikolai was working harder on these cases than ever before and his lack of appearances at home was evident.

Patricia looked about and in response, Dax Shandling pointed over to Jiri. Jiri stood to attention as his mother turned to lock her sights on her son.

He waited.

She beckoned him over enthusiastically. He approached with a gentle smile. She quietly placed the box on the ground and went in for a massive embrace. Jiri was all too keen to reciprocate. It seemed she was further out into the light than he anticipated.

'Sweet Jiri. I'm sorry about today.' Patricia said softly.

'It's okay Mother. Are we going home now or...?'

'If you can carry the box, I will hold your bicycle. I just need to have a final word with Dax about Reznik.'

'Do you know where he is, Mother?' Jiri asked, knowing full well she could know a lot more than he did despite her absence.

'I don't, but ... it's Reznik. You have to expect the unexpected. This was bound to happen sometime.'

'It's my fault.' Jiri conceded.

She handed Jiri the box and then carefully, she touched the top of his forehead and slid her cold finger down his nose.

A sign of love.

Jiri used the edge of the box to itch the tip of his nose and then smiled.

'Okay, Mother. I'll wait by the fountain.'

8

THE IVANOV APARTMENT

A WHILE LATER

Patricia left Jiri's bicycle in the area beneath the stairwell and then joined Jiri as he clambered up the steps, box in hand. Jiri narrowly avoided stepping on a black tile? as he made the turn at the first level corridor. Jiri couldn't see over the box, but even if he could, his eyes would be met with the dense spill of darkness, broken only by the carbon-filament light that shone from the middle stairwell opening. Night was settling in, but sleep was the last thing on Jiri's mind. All he could think about was finally having an evening in his apartment where his mother would be there, functioning as he knew she wanted to function. It could be weeks, even months before her next slip into darkness. The timings were always different. The grace period was therefore treasured. He didn't want to lose a moment of this time.

Just enjoy it ... while there was light, Jiri wanted everything to be right. There were gaps that he was glad would be omitted. Even his father didn't want to tell Patricia of the things that had gone wrong in her absence: Jiri's truancy, the incident at the apartment crime scene. She didn't need to feel guilt for not being there. As far as she was aware, everything was fine.

No sooner had they reached their floor than their return home was suddenly halted. Jiri saw it first and didn't know what to think. Patricia saw it, and even though she had no idea where it came from, she knew it was bad.

Very, very bad.

'What is that thing outside our apartment door?' Patricia asked Jiri.

Jiri froze. He recognised what it was from its form, its size, its material and design. He related it to something he didn't want to recall. He thought it came from his dream, but now he knew, it ... was ... real.

'It's a chair.' Jiri said. 'I've seen it before.'

Jiri placed the giftware box on the ground and for some reason, as he approached the grand armchair he felt a burning on his shoulder. Something stirred and his head began to throb.

Patricia put out a hand and stopped his advance.

'Wait! Don't go near it.'

'Mother?' Jiri asked. 'I've seen this armchair before.'

'I know ...' Patricia said ominously. Jiri looked at her with confusion and asked the obvious question.

'Have you seen that chair before?'

'I think so, Jiri. In my dreams, Jiri. Have you seen it before?'

'Yes.' Jiri said. 'I don't like it.'

Across the hall, a little way from the armchair, a ginger tomcat clawed at the door to Mr. Dolya's apartment. The door was shut, and probably locked. The cat was in distress, but neither Jiri nor Patricia wanted to get any closer. Neither of them wanted to knock on Mr. Dolya's door while that chair was still sat there.

'Jiri, we need to get into our apartment.' Patricia said. 'Hold my hand.'

Patricia and Jiri pressed up against the sidewall of the corridor, and carefully, they inched closer to the chair. Jiri's ears picked up a high-pitched resonance as they got closer and closer.

'Whatever you do, Jiri, don't touch it!'

'Mother?' Jiri asked in a whisper. 'How do you know about this chair?'

'Shhh.' Patricia hushed. They stopped as they arrived at the chair's side. There was no getting closer to it as long as they remained pressed against the wall. The chair grumbled at them. The vibrations that came were intense and jarring.

Patricia reached for her apartment door key, eyed up the lock on the door and pulled Jiri close behind. He felt the heat of the chair's presence on his back. Patricia turned the lock, turned the knob and pushed hard, and together they fell inside the apartment. Losing his balance, Jiri spilled onto the carpet runner while Patricia swung and skidded her feet inside with her hand still on the doorknob. Jiri got to his feet first, pulled his mother inside, and closed the door.

As he did, the slice of what he saw before the door closed sent a chill down his spine. He saw the chair from its side. He could have sworn he saw a hand resting on the arm of that chair, as if somebody had been sitting in it all this time.

Patricia staggered to her feet and brushed herself off.

'Did you see him?' She asked Jiri immediately noting Jiri's distant stare towards the door.

'Yes.' Jiri acknowledged. He then rattled his thoughts and shook his head. 'Wait … what?' he asked.

'Don't be afraid, Jiri.' Patricia turned her son to face her and gently knelt onto her knees. 'Just ghosts. Even inanimate objects have problems with letting go, sometimes.'

Jiri searched his thoughts and knew it to be true. He touched the chair when he was in the apartment. It had things it needed to show him. Things that it had not been able to forget.

'Objects aren't like people, Mother.'

'People are nature.' Patricia began to explain. 'Everything in existence has a special connection with the universe. All nature knows, remembers, and most importantly can recall what is important.'

Jiri couldn't take it all in. The explanation left him more confused than ever. He then looked about the ground and realised that they had arrived in the apartment empty-handed.

'We left the box in the corridor!'

'Don't panic, Jiri.' Patricia said as she took off her coat. Her face was serious once more. 'Your father will pick it up. I will look out for him at the window and warn him about that chair.'

Upon hearing the plan Jiri suddenly felt ridiculous. He started to snicker, but away from his mother's gaze. He couldn't muffle the sound however and knew it was wrong to laugh, but he couldn't help it. He separated the horror of the apartment with the idea that it was just a chair: nothing more and nothing less. He knew there was something dark behind it. He didn't need that drumming into him, but in that moment, it was just a chair.

'What's so funny, Jiri?' his mother said as she went over to the kitchen and lit the gas on the top of the stove with a match.

'What are we going to do now?' Jiri asked.

'We'll heat up some soup.'

'Mother!' Jiri pushed, but with a gentle smile she knew nothing else was his mind, nor was he capable of distraction.

'We have to ignore it, Jiri.' She said. 'Put our energy to ordinary things. Pretend it's not there. It's the only way that he won't get to us.'

'Mother. Who is Tobe Healy?' Jiri asked, confident she would know all.

She looked away. She was focused on pouring soup from a can into a pan.

'Is that his name?'

Jiri felt as though he and his mother had only just this moment realised that they were members of the same fan club. She was ironclad, however; she stuck to her guns and kept tight-lipped.

'Mother!' Jiri insisted.

Patricia sighed and whispered. 'Let's not do this while that chair is out there. Trust me. Be silent, be patient.'

She turned back and stirred the soup. Jiri stared at the front door and wondered how a chair could listen to him from so far away. If they could only whisper the quietest of all whispers…

He stared too much. The door began to growl — or at least the chair behind the door was letting him know that it was still there and that it was most definitely listening.

His mother was probably right. They should wait until Nikolai came home.

He would know what to do.

He always did.

8PM THAT NIGHT

Nikolai parked his car outside his home block after a brief diversion via Dax Shandling's home in the city. Dax had explained all that he knew about Reznik's disappearance. It turned out that Reznik had not returned home to his family that evening. Very unusual behaviour for a family man like Reznik. This meant that he was in some kind of trouble. Something deep.

Nikolai sat quietly in his car for a moment, still wondering how he was going to explain that to Patricia. Dax also explained that Patricia had visited the market during the day and that she was there to see to it that Reznik's and her items were going to the right place.

Talk about timing. Nikolai thought. Patricia's sixth sense about coming down to the market was also noted by Mr. Shandling. Questions about her "spooky behaviour" had always been posed, but shot down by Nikolai.

Nikolai had spent enough time away from home, and knowing that Patricia was out and about, he wanted to spend as much time as he could with her and Jiri. He feared these events were most likely going to put a damper on things.

#

Nikolai headed up the stairs, chasing a white snowball cat that walked slowly into the fourth-floor corridor. It ran along and sniffed at the object that sat in the middle of the corridor. The cat made an abrupt blood-curdling noise and retreated down the corridor into the darkness.

Nikolai halted immediately upon seeing the arm chair. His heart stopped and he forgot to breathe in for a moment. Nikolai charged down toward the chair. He felt nothing but a rumbling sound in his ears as he approached the chair. As he passed Mr. Dolya's front door he felt a great force grab hold of his shoulder. Nikolai was pulled back against Mr. Dolya's front door, which opened easily, as if somebody had pulled him back and opened it for him. With the apartment now open, Nikolai slipped and then staggered inside. Two cats jumped over his legs and the chair, hissed, and ran down the stairwell.

The apartment was in pitch-black darkness except for light from three candles that burned at the centre of his dining room table.

'Mr. Dolya?' He announced, noticing that whoever had pulled him into his apartment was not there.

Just cats.

A lot of cats. More than a dozen, that was for sure. Nikolai wondered if Mr. Dolya was hiding in his bedroom. Hiding perhaps because he too had come into contact with the chair and was shaken to his core. Perhaps Mr. Dolya didn't know what he was doing. If he could only come out and Nikolai would explain and gain further help from his good neighbour.

The bedroom door was ajar.

'Mr. Dolya? Are you in there?' Nikolai felt unsure if he wanted to go further. He checked behind the front door. Nobody hiding there. There weren't any other places to hide that were obvious, however ...

The window in Dolya's kitchenette was wide open, but not wide enough for a man of his size to get out of so quickly. Besides, there were cats coming in and out of there with such frequency, Nikolai didn't know if he'd seen the same cats again or if other new ones had made an appearance. Surely there couldn't be this many in the surrounding area where they lived.

Jiri took note of a newcomer; a long-haired grey stalked in, very wary of the other cats. It growled at them as it carried the corpse of a vole in its mouth. Nikolai approached the bedroom, two steps forward as the grey cat took a defensive stance. It was now growling, cowering at him now. Nikolai hissed back, but that got the attention of another one. A skinny black cat with large ears looked up at him and hissed back.

The long-haired grey cat jumped off the kitchenette counter and ran through the gap in the bedroom door with its jowls still full of sacrificial offerings.

Nikolai carried on forward.

'Mr. Dolya?' he said as he opened the bedroom door. The smell hit him first. The sight of the grey cat as it dropped the vole on the bed led his eye to what could only be described as a mass pile of death. As Nikola's eyes adjusted to what he was seeing, on the bed, from tip to toe, all he could see were the bloodied corpse of birds, mice and voles. It was the strangest thing that Nikolai had ever seen. The entire bed was covered with cat offerings of every avifaunal and crawling vermicular that could be caught and killed. The grey cat jumped off the bed and scuttled out through the door.

Although Nikolai was certain that Mr. Dolya was not anywhere underneath all the offerings, it was the strangest thing for sure to see so many cats, gravitating by their natural instincts to bring things to this one spot.

Whoever had pulled him into Mr. Dolya's apartment wasn't there. With that confirmed, Nikolai got out of that apartment as quickly as he could.

He closed the door and was once again presented with the problem of the armchair. He saw Jiri opening the door to the apartment slightly with curiosity.

'Stay back inside, Jiri. Close that door.'

'Okay, Papa.' Jiri replied.

Patricia replaced him at the gap of the door, casual and calm.

'Nikolai, what are you going to do?'

'I'm going to need help. I'll go down to the telephone and try and get Pavel to come down and help. Now please, if I were you, I'd close that door.'

The door started to close, but Nikolai felt a need to say one more thing.

'Patricia?'

The door opened and Patricia looked out questioningly.

'Yes?'

Nikolai then whispered, 'It's good to see you …'

Patricia smiled, 'It's good to see you too …'

#

Nikolai ran down to the nearest phone exchange box. He put out a call to the nearest phone and asked the receiver to give a message to Pavel who was at this time nowhere near a phone to talk to him directly.

Nikolai waited in the public phone box until Pavel got his call back to him announcing that he was on his way. Nikolai then went back up to engage in a staring contest with the armchair from a relatively safe distance until Pavel arrived. The chair looked back at him, and through the powers of pareidolia, the chair eventually looked back at him. The gaps between the arms and the back of the chair became down gazing eyes. The front lip of the cushion, which sat slightly raised from the base of the seat, became a sneering mouth. The longer he looked, the more he heard it growl. The sound of scratching from Mr. Dolya's door came and went in waves, which had to be chair-related behaviour. Animals sensed things far more intensely than humans.

The growling increased, or so it seemed. Nikolai reached into his jacket and pulled out his service revolver. He wondered: *Is this how Tobe Healy stays one step ahead?* Is he able to see memory from objects? Jiri had mentioned in his vocal ramblings that he saw a boot strike the chair where he stood. Perhaps violent actions against inanimate objects produced something of a marker. A memory. A vibration from such a strike would then stay with that object.

He then thought about why Tobe Healy wanted Patricia in the first place. He was after more than that. He wanted the complete set. Patricia was just the beginning. If he couldn't have her he would …

Nikolai stopped his thoughts. He didn't want to feed the room with anything more than what Tobe Healy may already know. Clear your mind … Nikolai thought as he closed his eyes and attempted to meditate. He sat on the carpet runner, ten meters away from the growing, sneering chair. The growling got louder as he tried to clear anything that could be used against him. When Nikolai felt as though he succeeded, he opened his eyes and said sternly,

'Shut up!'

The growling ceased immediately.

After a breath of silence a shadow loomed. The

sound of heavy boots tore through the air and the smell of cigarette smoke wafted in with Pavel Fleischaker who was hot and flustered from the climb up the stairs. Nikolai stood and shook his sweaty hand.

'Nikolai. What on earth are you doing sitting out here in the dark?' Pavel said.

'I have a bit of a problem.' Nikolai pointed down at the chair.

'Nikolai. It's an armchair.'

'Not just any chair.'

'Oh... it's THE armchair?'

'Yes. It is that armchair ...' Nikolai then whispered. 'I don't know how it got here.'

'It was taken from the house and put in storage. How did it end up here?'

'I do not know.'

After several beats, Pavel asked, 'What do you want me to do?'

'I can't go near it. I want you to take that bloody thing miles from here, and I want you to smash it up. Burn it.'

'Voodoo shit. All this mystical crap is beyond me.' Pavel admitted. 'But while it's here, why don't you get Jiri to sit on it. See what he sees. I want to see some magic tricks. Prove you right, prove you—'

'Not a chance.' Nikolai interrupted. 'This is Tobe's way out. It's not a two-way situation.'

'You know for sure?'

Nikolai pulled Pavel away to the stairwell.

'Listen to me. That chair gives Healy a direct portal to my family. This is how he leads and likely why they are always following in his wake. I don't know how it got here, but it's dangerous. I need you to help me. Too many things are happening, and I don't think any of it is a coincidence.'

Pavel grunted. 'Fine, I'll do it. A chair can't hurt me.' Pavel moved away and down the corridor in a whirlwind of might and intent. He took a hold of the chair and then stopped, frozen. Nikolai watched for a moment. Pavel wasn't moving.

'Oh no.' Pavel said as he dropped ash on the chair's seat.

Nikolai reached for his gun.

'What is it, Pavel?'

Pavel turned to face Nikolai. His eyes full of …

Jest. With a smile Pavel said, 'I just remembered, I didn't leave the car running. It's going to take a while to turn that engine over in the cold.'

Nikolai shook his head. Pavel laughed a malicious laugh as he lifted the armchair and started down the corridor with it in hand. All of a sudden, the chair was nothing more than a household spider in a bathtub that Nikolai was too scared to handle himself.

'I know where to take this thing. Don't you worry. I won't tell anybody you called me in the dead of night to move furniture.'

Nikolai headed up the staircase so that he could give distance between himself and Pavel as he carried the chair down on his back. It was effortless. It was easy.

It was humiliating to say the least.

'I'll see you in the morning Nikolai!' Pavel hollered back.

'Thank you Pavel. This means a lot.'

Nikolai returned to the now empty corridor to see Jiri opening Mr. Dolya's apartment door.

'Jiri, stay away from there!' Nikolai called out as he charged down the corridor. Cats spilled out in droves, all of them sniffed about then scattered in all directions.

Nikolai stopped and then touched the ground where the chair sat and felt nothing of significance. He looked at Jiri, frozen at the mouth of Mr. Dolya's door.

'Wow, Mr. Dolya's got a massive cat problem.' Jiri announced. As he turned to see his father's reaction, Mr. Dolya's door slammed shut.

Jiri let out a yelp and stared at his father, aghast at the sudden event. They both remained silent until Nikolai had chewed over the possible explanations.

'Must have been a gust of wind, Jiri.'

Jiri nodded. Another door opened, this time it was the Ivanov apartment. Patricia peered out from the hand-closed door, having overheard the discussion thus far.

'Why don't you both come in, get some food and we can talk about this. Mr. Dolya will no doubt whistle his way home and we will all hear him.'

'Food would be good.' Nikolai smiled meekly

knowing full well that he'd skipped food for pretty much the entire day. Eating was never a priority when you are sick with worry, but having Patricia suggest it, in clarity, and in the light of her regular self, how could he ignore the pangs that pinched and ached?

Yes. He thought. *It was a very good idea indeed.*

9

THE IVANOV APARTMENT

LATER

It was long past midnight. Nobody wanted to sleep. Jiri had curled up in front of the wood fire with his mother who very contentedly curled his hair. She drank tea while Nikolai sipped vodka, trying his hardest to unwind. Jiri and Patricia had talked about what happened after he played truant. Patricia was unsettled about Nikolai's explanation of why he had taken Jiri to a crime scene knowing full well that the killer, L'assassino di nota, was out there on the prowl, but she realised that may have been the only alternative.

Like Jiri had originally thought, she also felt guilty.

She should have been the alternative.

'I don't want you to be sorry, Patricia.' Nikolai conceded. 'It's my fault, and it will be my cross to bear.'

'You don't need to go that far.' Patricia said as she extended her hand to meet his. 'Everything happens for a reason. At least we know his name. His real name: Tobe Healy.'

'I don't like hearing that.' Jiri said. 'Why is he doing this to us?'

Nikolai sat up and placed his empty glass on his table.

'No matter, I've got to run this to its conclusion. The only end I'm willing to accept is his capture and exec …'

'Nikolai!' Patricia swallowed Nikolai's words for the sake of Jiri's ears. 'I don't think he needs to know any more than he already '

'Oh I think we've already passed that marker. It's time he knew.'

Jiri knew they were talking about him. He already had pretty much an idea about what was going on in terms of their being in some kind of danger. He had grown up in post-war Prague. Not a lot of things were kept hidden. He believed he was tough-skinned, or at least, he hoped he was in this case. Despite her protective instincts, Patricia nodded. 'He's a smart boy. Not knowing would surely drive him crazy. He needs to be prepared. On guard!'

Jiri too sat at attention. 'I'm right here. You can

talk to me. I can handle myself, Mother, Father …' He then slipped off his mother's chair and went to sit closer to the fire so he could capture both his parents' attention. 'Tell me.'

Nikolai locked eyes with Jiri, and soon he figured out where to begin.

'It is safe to say that if it wasn't for him, that your mother and I would never have met.'

'Perhaps under better circumstances Nikolai.' Patricia added with a softened smile.

'Yes.' Nikolai said returning the smile. 'You know your mother is from Italy, right? Well, when she was a young adult, she was taken from her family.'

'Taken by Healy?' Jiri asked.

'L'assassino di nota.' Nikolai nodded. 'She was taken to a remote island off the shores of Venice where Healy kept her in captivity. Because I was the best in my field, I was ordered across to help with the Italian police. I was the one who found her. Liberated her.'

'Who is Healy?' Jiri asked. "Why did he want Mother so badly?'

'Let me be clear. Healy … Healy is a killer who used strange forces of nature to get away with murder. Your mother however has an ability to see things. That's why Healy wanted her so badly. Her and others like her.'

Patricia pursed her lips at Nikolai, not wanting him to add any more to that. There was still a pressing need to be discreet. They also still didn't want Jiri to know everything. To know some things would ultimately put his life in danger.

'In fact, after we saved your mother, she came with me on several unrelated cases. We became quite the team.'

'More than just a team.' Patricia said.

'But soon enough we realised that the cases soon became all about Healy again. He was still out there, and he used the killings to get our attention. He was trying to get at your mother again. So we had no choice but to leave Italy. I brought her here so I could keep her safe.'

Patricia spoke softly to Jiri. It was almost as if she were telling him a fable. A fairy tale. 'We went through the war like warriors! We were allowed to live. But still, after those hard times came these times of change. After the war, we were all in a better place. We had you, and things were safe.'

'But we're not safe.' Jiri replied. 'Why don't we leave here, and go away, far away so Healy can't find you again?'

'It's not that simple, Jiri.' Nikolai said. 'I mean here, I have my place. We have our badge of protection. The StB and the VB police surround us. They are on our side. We could never have this level of protection anywhere else in the world. Not without starting from the very bottom.'

'But things are different now.' Jiri said.

'You're right.' Nikolai said, 'Things are different, but Healy wouldn't do this unless we were close. He wouldn't make himself known if he didn't feel threatened.'

Patricia then added with a question, 'But we are close, aren't we?'

Nikolai did not answer. The only thing that had changed was that Jiri had contact with Healy directly. That meant that he now knows that Jiri has a quality similar to Patricia's, if not stronger. Jiri thought about things for a while and he too came to the same conclusion.

'He's after me now? Isn't he?' The apartment was silent. Jiri continued, 'This is all my fault.'

'Don't say that again, Jiri, do you hear?' Nikolai chastised harshly, but he didn't mean to. He was talking out of his own guilt; after all, he had put Jiri in that situation. He was led right to Healy's well-placed trap.

Patricia stood and headed over to the window.

'Nikolai, can you promise that we're going to get him? Please, we must know that we're going to get him before he gets to us.'

Nikolai rubbed his face with both hands. He wanted to promise but there were too many things happening out of his control.

Jiri's eyes widened suddenly. He had a thought. Another line was connecting the dots.

'Reznik Killian went missing today, father, could he ... I mean ...'

Nikolai stood wearily. 'I know. But that can't have anything to do with this ...' He waved his hands dismissively.

'Maybe not.' Patricia said. 'But the chair that Jiri

saw at that crime scene was just down the hall. Who put that there, Nikolai?'

'You're right. Things have moved on fast, but these have to be desperate moves from Healy. He doesn't have a chance against an entire police force. We have protection. I can arrange it in an instant if needed.' Nikolai offered up all that he could to ensure their safety. If he had to.

'Mr. Dolya hasn't whistled home yet either,' Jiri added.

'Perhaps he's just out of town. The cats' behaviour was because of the arm chair. I know that for sure.' Nikolai recalled the feeling of being pulled into Mr. Dolya's apartment door. He still hadn't managed to explain that, nor was a gust of wind a reasonable explanation for the door's timely closing. 'I wouldn't have known if his apartment door was left unlocked if it weren't for that chair. Perhaps he doesn't lock it at all. Or maybe he forgot…

Jiri walked over to the window. He wanted to be the first to hear Mr. Dolya arrive back. He looked out to the street below and watched as commuters passed by in cars and on foot. Jiri shifted his gaze as a tram moved up through the gaps of the side street that lead to the main road, and in the distance, he saw the famous bridges that made Prague a magnificent sight.

Patricia and Nikolai sat together on the couch. She sighed heavily.

'I don't think it's a coincidence that all of this

happened after Jiri touched that chair. Do you?'

'He barely touched it before he fell under.' Nikolai stated.

'It's long enough. Now Healy ... Healy is acting out. The chair, Reznik ... and maybe even Mr. Dolya.' Patricia's eyes widened. 'Nikolai, I can feel that everything is connected.'

'Are you sure about the Reznik thing. I mean, he's a buffoon with many problems. This was bound to happen, right?' Nikolai asked with a cautious sense of trust. She was never wrong. 'I mean we can't be sure that these events mean anything. They might just be distractions ... If he didn't want Jiri, or you, what did he really want?'

'This has always been about ...' Patricia whispered in Nikolai's ear, 'Three sisters.'

Jiri could barely hear her, but he could see her lips move. His father followed suit, whispering with his mouth away so Jiri couldn't see what he was saying ...

Jiri stared at his mother for a few moments as sadness filled her eyes. He heard a voice.

Jiri ...

His name was being called. It was not from inside the room, nor was it in his head. Down on the street below Jiri saw the unmistakable hand movement from what appeared to be an exasperated Mr. Dax Shandling.

The local chairman of the marketing community took a moment to rest his heavy bulk, bending over double with hands on knees in sheer exhaustion.

His car was parked a little away down the road, half off the curb as if he had stopped in some kind of a deranged state. Dax looked up again and shouted.

'Jiri! Go for your father. Please!' The desperation in the man's voice was clear, and Jiri reached to open the window and called for his father to come.

Nikolai arrived at the window and saw the withered look on Mr. Shandling's face.

'It's Mr. Killian. I saw him through his window. It's …. Mr. —' Dax said scraping to a wheeze which then turned into explosive coughing.

'I'm on my way down.' Nikolai called.

Jiri stood to attention as he watched his father heading for the door. Off he goes again … He'd not even managed to take his coat and scarf off. He barely managed to appreciate the change in Patricia, mother and wife. Jiri knew that this was important, but for some reason he didn't want him to go. It was a feeling Jiri had never felt before. A dark lingering whisper in his head said it was not safe.

'Father, please, stay. Don't go!' Jiri insisted as he went to pull off one of his father's black leather gloves. In doing so, his notepad fell to ground. Nikolai didn't see it, for he was too busy with the recovery of his glove to the correct fingers. He then gestured for calm.

'I can't just say no. Every lead is a step closer to ending Healy's reign of terror. I have to do this.'

Usually, Patricia would never say anything that

would jinx Nikolai on his exit for work. Superstition was indeed present in her culture and in her family; but as she stooped down and held Jiri, she gazed up at Nikolai and whispered...

Go get him.'

'I will.' Nikolai smiled grimly. He looked at Jiri and nodded. 'I'm sorry, son.'

Jiri watched as his father left the apartment. The feeling of finality came over him.

'It is okay, Jiri, you stay with me.' His mother smiled weakly. Jiri heard a twinge ... or more so ... a raw shakiness to her words. He looked her in the eye and tried hard to stare deeply, as if he could know for sure what she he was sensing. Your father knows what he's doing. She said without moving her lips.

Jiri frowned. It was not the first time he'd heard voices lingering in the air beyond that of his own thoughts or imaginings.

With his father gone, he sat quietly waiting. His mother looked out of the window, perhaps seeing Nikolai as he hit the road with Dax Shandling.

It was then that Jiri noticed his father's notebook. He'd left it behind. Father never left without his notebook. It sat on the ground at the side of the couch. He went to pick it up and opened it. He had seen his father open and take notes and even just read it through many times, but he had never once carried enough curiosity to look at its contents.

Perhaps the very thought of it worried Jiri. He

picked it up nonetheless and sat with it on the couch. His mother wrapped her arm around him. She looked down approving of his having the notepad. He opened it.

The pages were blank ...

He turned pages and still, they were blank. It was the same book. The cover was dog eaten and worn. There was no chance that it was a new ... there had only, as far as Jiri could remember, only been one notebook.

Suddenly on a page, words appeared - as if they'd been missed, and he'd only just noticed them.

Keep this notebook safe, Jiri. For your father's sake and for ours, keep it safe.

Jiri was astonished. Who wrote this? He looked up at his mother as she stood dreamily staring out of the window. She was humming a song. A song she only ever sang in her dark state. The humming ceased, she turned her head to Jiri, and very simply, saying nothing, she nodded.

10

PRAGUE - OUTER LIMITS

Nikolai sat next to a pensive, if not visually disturbed, Dax Shandling as he gave directions along one of the many narrow one-track country roads that trailed beyond the boundaries of Prague. Trees became dense and the lights of the city fell behind. There was nothing but a solid sheet of darkness ahead. The snow appeared sparse and light. Farmhouse gas lamps carried the glow within the little recesses of driveways along a less beaten path. The car beams dipped low. It couldn't have felt more isolated. Mr. Shandling had already been down this road alone at night, seen whatever he'd seen at Reznik's place, and driven all the way back to the city.

'I was here, sitting with Reznik's wife only a few

hours before ...' Dax asked.

'What exactly did you see?' Nikolai said.

'Whatever happened, it was within the last three hours.' Dax's voice began to shake. 'She was alive, and we spoke. She was worried. I told her everything was going to be okay. I said I'd check back on them when I came through again. I only left them for three hours. I told her she would be okay ... Whoever did this must have been waiting for me to leave ...' Dax hit the dash and snapped with rage.

'What do you mean?' Nikolai pressed. 'What did you see?' Nikolai asked, although half expecting to not get a clear answer. From the look of Mr. Shandling's face, he was uncomfortable enough as it was. He swallowed and gave his all.

'Glass ...' Dax said, short and to the point. 'Blood and glass!'

Dax shook his head, not exactly understanding what to say further. Nikolai held back his personal thoughts. If this was anything to do with Healy, it was going to be nasty, even more than it had before. Even though he'd seen a lot of bad things, the worst was always waiting for him around the corner. Dax was getting more wound up the closer they got to the Killian house, but Nikolai had to have a picture of what he was walking into.

'What about his family? You mentioned his wife? What about the children?'

Dax shifted in his seat and peered out of the side window.

'That's it! Right there.' He took a deep breath, a moment for pause. That was shortly followed by a shaky exhale and no further answers came from his now tight, quivering lips.

Nikolai stopped the car and looked over to the isolated lowly house surrounded by sheltered barns and chicken coops. Spare tires, wheel arches, and other remnants of cars were scattered about the land. The house was an old simple two-floor barn house, no doubt made of the tough stuff, having already out outlived the turmoil of recent times. Although beset within dense trees and darkness, one window was illuminated by candlelight — an upstairs bedroom perhaps.

Nikolai cranked down the window, and to his surprise, he could hear the faint sound of music: a dramatic patriotic gramophone recording of a male choir, all singing in Russian.

Nikolai looked at the blank expression on Dax's face. He seemed speechless.

'Was this how you found —?'

He didn't need to finish his sentence. Dax shook his head. 'There wasn't any music playing when I was here before. There weren't any candles.' Again he shook his head. His anxieties were high. He could barely look beyond the dashboard of the car.

Nikolai looked at the passenger seat, but he didn't see his notebook. He felt inside his jacket, but didn't find it in there either. He dismissed it — had to do without it this time — and made sure his gun was loaded, ready for anything and nothing at all.

'Are you coming in, or staying here?' Nikolai asked Dax, already knowing the answer.

'If you don't mind — '

Nikolai nodded and said, 'Keep the engine running. I will be back ...' as he exited the vehicle, he felt the chill in the midnight air. The countryside that surrounded them was eerily quiet and still. Nikolai looked towards the second barn. Its doors were half open. Nothing out of the ordinary about that, only for some reason, because of details, he made sure he remembered how the doors sat slightly open. He noted any objects that might appear out of place. Nothing stood out, and no matter how wary he was about being watched, he carried on forward, around to the side door into the main house, which was already wide open.

The music continued to play.

Inside the kitchen, light was limited to a single tea light which illuminated what appeared to be a freshly made bowl of soup on the old wooden kitchen table. The soup was still steaming hot. This was another sure sign that somebody had been here after Dax's first visit, or perhaps, that person had never actually left at all. Straightaway Nikolai knew that it pointed to one person: Tobe Healy. He had already set up scenes similar to this, as if leading the way through with sign posts.

Fresh heat on a cold case: He'd played this trick once before but never in plain sight. Darkness and light. Nikolai thought, this was what he was playing with ... Darkness and the light ... hot and cold.

A weird smell hung in the air. He looked at the floor and could see trails. It was blood. The trails started at the stove, dripped down and led all the way to the side door, and, he imagined, beyond, although he had not noticed any trails on the outside.

Darkness and light. He wasn't supposed to notice it until he was inside. He headed to the stove in the kitchen. He removed the lid of the pan and straight away, he gagged, threw the lid down with a clatter, and covered his mouth.

This was no ordinary soup. It was merely hot water and some kind of animal or even human bodily fluids. He very quickly reached for a tea towel and covered the bowl.

'Damn it.' He cursed himself for Healy must have planned this. Surely, he was drawn to the bowl on the table, but the pot on the stove had been left there to be found. Of course, he had to drop the pan lid. It made a noise – or more, it created a signal. That was his cue to let somebody know he was here.

Sure enough, through the darkness, Nikolai saw movement, beyond the kitchen, through the hallway towards the stairwell. What he saw — or thought he saw — was the flicker of a shadow that moved, and then lingered before disappearing upwards.

Nikolai drew his gun, and started towards the

hallway.

The music was still playing up on the first floor. Music planned only to draw him in.

There no hiding from Healy's game, Nikolai thought as he left the kitchen and headed slowly upwards without fear or consideration for what he was about to find. He tracked the upstairs candle light to its origin, and was surprised to see that now there was more than one candle. Tea lights had been lit across the floor, giving mixed feelings of romance and the occult.

This was where the music played.

Darkness, light, silence and sound ... Nikolai tried to hone in on something. Patterns meant everything and he knew they meant even more to Healy.

The gramophone was halfway through a complete recording, all in Russian. Nikolai carefully knocked off the needle, scratching it and creating an audible blemish that cut to an ear-popping silence.

That was all for that room. No reason to stay, especially now that another bad smell alerted Nikolai to search another room, even though all the other doors were shut tight apart from this one that had windows that faced the road.

Did Dax go all the way up here to find Reznik? He thought, realising that he should have asked which room he'd found him. All evidence pointed to that top window which turned out to be nothing but a beacon. Sure enough, there really was no other way. Dax must have been oblivious. Naïveté put a stop to his curiosity. This must have messed Mr. Shandling up more than he realised.

The top landing was dark and vacant of dark shadows or movement. The only thing that led him was his nose. The smell, similar to that of the flesh and bile broth from the kitchen, was again evident beyond one of the doors. Nikolai stood with his gun raised. He reached for the handle and slowly opened the door. The hinge scraped and whined as it opened.

Nikolai entered a room scented thick with death and flesh. The room was filled with large unlit church candles. Whether Healy had intended to have them lit was another question.

In the middle of the room on the floor was a shape: The unmistakable body of Reznik became clear in all its gory detail. The tall church candles had been wax fixed to the ground — a lot of wax had been melted to make them stand up on their own accord. A lot of time was spent in this. It couldn't have happened within three hours like Dax had said.

Nikolai dwelled on the detail. From head to toe, Reznik was covered in long shards of glass — fake Venetian vase shards. Every piece had been wedged into his flesh. The spectacle was truly unreal. Not one inch of his body was missed, right down to his hands where smaller parts of his glass trinkets had been inserted into his skin, all standing upright like an experimental Art Deco piece in a provocative gallery that had gone too far.

The bloody corpse beneath all the glass shards of many colours was a complete mass of flesh. It was then that Nikolai realized that Reznik had been stripped naked before the act had even started. Whether or not he was alive when the first shards were inserted, Nikolai could not tell. From the facial expression on Reznik's face, he lived his last moments in excruciating pain, and Nikolai could hear the screams in his head.

The screams were as loud as the music that was playing again in the next room …

'Music?' Nikolai said. He took to his feet. He was certain he'd turned that player off. He even remembered the needle as it bounced off the gramophone record and into station keeping.

Somebody else was in the house with him. No doubt!

Nikolai stepped away from Reznik's glass covered corpse, turned with his gun held at relative eye level and ran to the other room with the music. He saw the gramophone playing as it was before. He saw another change; the window had now been opened. He ran like the wind down the staircase and through the kitchen.

Outside in the cold clear air, he saw the shape of a form running towards the barn. He gave chase.

'Dax?' Nikolai yelled. He turned to the car, noticing that Dax was still sitting inside, staring at him with bulging eyes out of the side window.

Scared shitless.

'You stay right there.' Nikolai called out. He didn't wait for Dax to acknowledge him. Nikolai turned back to the barn. The doors had been flung wide. He entered slowly to find a lamp glowing at the far back amongst the stacks of bailed hay. This was a backlight to illuminate the subtle shapes of two people that hung from rope that had been wrenched around their necks. Two bodies.

A woman and a child.

'Gottverdammt!' Nikolai exclaimed as he saw that their bowels were hanging out of their clothes ... still dripping.

That was the trail. The trail from the kitchen. The soup on the stove and the soup in the bowl ...

Nikolai looked at every corner of the barn. He felt a shadow pass behind him. He turned, looked out of the barn and saw something move past the car. Nikolai once again gave chase. He ran as fast as he could until he found himself slamming onto the bonnet of the car. He looked in where Dax had been before, but saw nothing but empty seats.

'Dax?' Nikolai bellowed to the dark surroundings. He walked around the car and checked down low in case he was cowering against a wheel, or something, while at the same time, he kept his eyes peeled for any other signs of movement in the near dark of night. Dax was nowhere to be seen and Nikolai didn't dare call out his name again.

Looking back at the house Nikolai saw now that

the room where Reznik lay dead was now clearly visible from the upstairs side window. He walked back slowly, staring up at something that reflected onto the ceiling of the room where Reznik's body lay still. The candles that surrounded Reznik's body had now been lit.

Another change ...

The candle light projected a subtle reflection onto the ceiling.

Nikolai gasped. He moved forward so he could see the manifestation clearly for himself. The shards of glass on Reznik's body had not been placed about the body by accident. The candlelight reflected a word on that workroom ceiling, so clearly spelling the words:

IT ALL ENDS WITH JIRI.

Oh no... what an intricate and frightful message it was to see, but Nikolai had known it ever since Jiri blacked out in that apartment where Healy had been. That moment changed everything.

Nikolai ran back to the car shouting once more 'Dax! I am leaving!' as loud as he could muster. There was again no return answer, or movement. The surrounding fields, woodland, roadside, and house were all frozen like a crime-scene photograph with nothing left to offer.

Nikolai jumped into the driver's seat and closed the door. He started the car engine. He couldn't stop looking for a sign. Anything at all that would force his hand and keep him there longer.

'Dax? I'm leaving. Right now...'

Nikolai waited a few beats of his heart longer before he pulled away from the side and back onto the country road.

Nikolai's thoughts were racing as fast as his heart beat. He had to forget Reznik and his family for they couldn't be helped. Patricia and Jiri were now foremost on his mind. It was time to take them away from here, get them away from the apartment. Things had changed. There was no longer a sense of protection, control, or certainty. Healy was ready, as if he'd been waiting far too long. Nikolai truly believed he was ahead of Tobe. But he had to have been there, on foot, at Reznik's house. They were as close as they'd ever gotten. Tobe Healy wasn't about to be caught or killed. He was a phantom. There would be no way of finding him out there in the dark on his own. No chance. Healy was going to go after Jiri and ... without a doubt.

11

DAX SHANDLING'S PLACE

PRAGUE - OUTER LIMITS

A shadow watched as Nikolai ran on foot from the house, towards the car at speed. The shadow waited until he fled into the darkness that surrounded the house of Reznik Killian. The shadow waited until he was clear and out of sight before he returned to the property that Nikolai had just visited.

First, the shadow paid a visit to the main barn, where he strolled past the hanging bodies. He needed to keep the barn fresh and untainted, so he left it how he found it.

The shadow retrieved several canisters of gasoline. He carried them calmly into the house. He started from the upstairs room where Reznik Killian's body lay, still glistening in the light of the tapered candles. He blew out the candles before generously pouring the gasoline over the body. The shadow took his time. He then took a hardcover book, which lay on a nearby desk, and with it, he smashed the window forcefully until there was nothing left but the frames. He went on to pour the gasoline about the rest of the room and on through to the top landing and then returned to the outhouse for two more canisters of gasoline.

Three return journeys later, he walked into the room filled with candles and the gramophone, which still blared out patriotic songs. He blew out the candles and continued to pour the gasoline, creating a clear circle around the gramophone as it finished its run. The needle settled to a stop. The shadow lifted the arm and restarted the symphony … one last time.

He headed downstairs and took a bottle of vodka from Reznik's private stash. The shadow knew all about Reznik and his house, his life and his secrets. The shadow knew a lot.

He carried the bottle outside, and took several swigs from it before he stuffed the neck with a rag, and lit it with a match. He threw it into the open window where Reznik lay. The rush of fire that followed was relentless and unforgiving.

The shadow stood satisfied. He had done exactly what Tobe Healy asked of him. He took cigarette from his jacket pocket and was ready to strike a match. He would have gone through with it if it wasn't for the gasoline soaked hands.

He grunted, and then smirked over the stupidity. He put the cigarette back into his pocket.

12

PRAGUE - OUTER LIMITS

EX POST FACTO

Nikolai floored the accelerator as hard as he could. To him, this single track that led back to the city seemed to go on forever. Within moments he noticed that the engine was spluttering, and the speedometer was dropping. He forced his foot against the accelerator even though it had already reached maximum bite. The wrenching sound from the engine was persistent. The vehicle rattled as if it were coming apart at the seams.

Nikolai could see the dim glow of fire, candles, oil lamps, and electricity in the far distance. Jiri was amongst that light. Nikolai felt the shroud of darkness flooding behind him like a giant oil spill.

The feeling spread thick and fast trying with all its might. What was left behind was trying to consume him. His family would be next.

To ask why Healy decided to kill Reznik was a no- brainer: he needed a body to deliver a message: The Venetian glass that had been wedged in every centimetre of Reznik's body was a call-back to Venice. It was letting Nikolai know that everything that connected to Patricia was at risk, including Jiri.

To Healy, Patricia was a treasure trove of hidden insight. Taking her didn't work. Pulling her world apart around her wasn't working either. But now, he knew how to get to her by going through Jiri. That would unlock all her secrets. Healy had always been patient.

That patience had worn out.

Before Nikolai could dig any further deeper into his assumptions, the car engine started to splutter and slow down, and fast. The fuel indicator pin had sunk below the empty line.

As the car ground to a halt, Nikolai took no time to curse or stress. He knew there had to be more gas in the trunk; there was a whole canister in there for sure. No car owner in their right mind would be without emergency fuel. He ran to the rear of the car and cranked open the trunk. With arms out stretched ready to reach for the canister, a mirror of an arm flopped out to greet him. Nikolai gasped and froze. After a fleeting moment of concern, he reached in and lifted the twisted, bloodied, and eye-popped head of Dax Shandling that lay separate from his body. The rest of him was cold and wet, so the killing had happened in the snow, right outside of Reznik Killian's house.

In fact, Nikolai realized he had seen it happen. He remembered when he headed to the barn with his gun out stretched, the image of Dax staring at him from the window of the car. His eyes were bulging then, but Nikolai hadn't put two and two together. He had thought Dax was just acting on what was going on outside of the car, but now, it was obvious that he was more concerned about what had a hold on him inside the car. His eyes were bulging because somebody had him by the throat ... literally.

Nikolai had missed it. It was too late for afterthoughts.

There was no time to dwell.

No time to dwell.

There was no gasoline canister. Everything but Dax and the spare tire was left. This was not getting him any closer to Jiri.

'Damn you Healy ...' Nikolai slammed the trunk shut and raised his hands, brushed his hair back with the strain of not knowing what to do.

Nikolai listened.

There was something underneath the car. He looked down at the road at his feet and noticed a steady drizzle of gasoline trailing its way onto the snow covered road surface.

Nikolai followed the sporadic trail for as far

back as the eye could see. Looking beneath the car, he saw a screwdriver wedged deep into the tank. Fuel dripped from its handle. The road beneath the screwdriver was a constant drip of fuel.

'No... No...!' Nikolai exclaimed as he struck his hands against the car. He rose to his feet. He saw something new from behind, in the distance, from where he'd just been. The dark road back to Reznik Killian's place was glowing, rising with the approaching beams of a car light.

Nikolai didn't believe in coincidences. He knew for a fact that this was not going to be just any random driver. He had to, however, take a chance. If it was he would need to make the vehicle stop and demand to be taken into the city. The approaching Skoda 1102 was familiar. One of the larger classes of vehicles bought from a do-up graveyard, abandoned by one of the German high commanders who left Prague in a hurry at the end of the war.

As the slowed down, Nikolai readied his pistol carefully behind his back and shielded the light from the car beams with his other hand.

Suddenly he realized that everything about this was wrong. Very little time went by before the driver confidently stepped out from the vehicle. The engine was left running, and the lights kept the mystery driver in complete darkness — three things that straightaway told Nikolai to reach for his weapon.

The arm of the driver rose up and levelled with

Nikolai' head.

The sound of gunfire pierced the silence.

The bullet, like a wrecking ball, struck Nikolai's shoulder blade. He took the brunt and remained standing in absolute shock, with nothing but the sound of dense ringing in his ears. His head felt disconnected from his entire body. Nikolai had enough in him to raise his own service revolver and pull the trigger. Just once. The sound of glass shattered and the tungsten light of the vehicle in front of him died along with it. Silence followed as Nikolai hit the ground.

Instantly, he shivered with a cold that both surrounded him and stunned every muscle, scraping along the core of every bone. Nikolai could see a face hovering over him and the smell of gasoline wafted from the driver's clothing.

The gun once again loomed into his eyeline. That gun barrel was the last thing that Nikolai ever saw. The smell of gasoline, however, lingered.

13

THE IVANOV APARTMENT

THE NEXT MORNING

Jiri was asleep. How he was asleep was a mystery. He didn't dream. He didn't feel or sense anything unusual in the night. He just slept in complete darkness within his own bedcovers and blankets.

Patricia looked out of the window as dawn arrived along with a brilliant fog. She could only just see the pavement below, and then moments later, the car that pulled up in front of the apartment block.

Her heart sank as two StB officers left the vehicle and headed inside. She did not know who they were, nor did she know why they were here.

Oh, that was a lie.

She knew something wasn't right. There were far too many promises. Far too many things said before Nikolai left that made the arrival of two anonymous StB officers inevitable. Patricia let them into the apartment, both of them wore solemn faces. She sat down. It was easier, she thought, to hear bad news sitting down.

The words, Nikolai, your husband, and dead all came in the same sentence. The world went silent. Her stomach knotted and everything about her physicality tightened. She was lost in her mind again. The two StB officers were still talking, but there was no seeing or hearing them at all. Not now that she knew that Nikolai, your husband is dead.

Nikolai, your husband is dead.

Nikolai, your husband...

Jiri's father...

Patricia immediately ran into Jiri's room and hugged him, smelt his hair, felt him breathe, as if it was the only thing that existed of Nikolai. Jiri awoke suddenly as she started to howl the inconsolable howls that he had only ever heard from behind her bedroom door. Much to Jiri's horror, she held him so tight that the StB agents, upon hearing Jiri struggle for breath ran in and pulled Patricia away from him.

This did not go down well with Patricia.

Jiri sat on the bed stunned — and still very much in the dark — as his mother started to writhe wildly on the ground. Another officer who was waiting outside the apartment came in to restrain her. Within the yelling and anguish were words that he didn't want to believe.

He's dead... he got him... he's dead!

They dragged her out of Jiri's room and closed the door. She struggled and she tried her hardest to bite her way free. Minutes went by and she finally found the couch where she sobbed. She curled up and churned out unknown words as she pulled at her own hair.

'He got him, he's really dead... he got him... he's going to get us too... he... got... him!' she yelled. Jiri listened against the bedroom door. He knew what that meant. He felt nothing. It wasn't like anything he'd ever heard before. His father would have to come home soon and explain to his mother that he's not really dead.

Jiri listened as one officer then said to the other, 'We've got to get her out of here.'

'I have orders to wait for Pavel.' said the other StB officer.

'What about the boy?' one officer said.

'Be quiet and hold her down!' the other interrupted. His mother screamed as one held her while the other injected her. Within minutes, all was silent.

'I told you that's how she'd react.' the other said.

'The boy is still in the room...' one officer said.

'Pavel said to wait. He will deal with the boy.'

Jiri ran to the window. He looked out and saw that the drop was far too high. There was no fire escape on their side of the building — a thoughtless oversight.

But there was a way out from Mr. Dolya's apartment.

Jiri waited, but saw his chance to get past the StB officers came and went as more men arrived — this time in white coats. Jiri watched through the crack in the door as his mother was placed on a gurney.

Another man arrived. A smartly dressed man with round-framed glasses who barked instructions to the men wearing white who carefully carried Jiri's now-sleeping mother out of the apartment.

When he realised his mother was being taken away, Jiri suddenly sprang to action. He ran out to the side of the stretcher. He tugged back and forced one of the carriers to stop in his tracks.

'Where are you taking my mother?' Jiri asked.

'Let go of the stretcher, boy.' the carrier in the white coat said. The argument and the tussle with the stretcher carried on into the corridor. Jiri's angst and struggle heightened the further away they got from their home.

'You're not taking her. You're not taking her.' He yelled.

'Get off the stretcher!'

The man with the round-framed glasses told the medic otherwise. 'Let the boy go with his mother.'

One of the StB officers protested. 'Excuse me, Doctor, but Inspector Pavel Fleischaker gave us strict instructions to keep the boy here. His mother is clearly a danger to herself, especially now that nobody is here to take care of her.'

Jiri was enraged, 'She's my mother! I will take care of her!'

The doctor pulled Jiri away from the gurney. He kicked and he screamed. He watched as the gurney with his mother —unconscious yet still brutally restrained — was carried away

'Go back inside your apartment.' The other StB officer said as he stood in his way like a wall that couldn't be brought down, no matter how hard Jiri hit back.

Jiri waited until his mother slipped out of sight before stealing across to Mr. Dolya's apartment. He knew the door to that apartment was not locked.

Luck had it that a cat brushed past the ankles of the StB officer. He looked down, and as the cat sprinted down the corridor, the other StB officer left the Ivanov apartment.

Jiri was no longer in the corridor.

The officers questioned the status of Mrs. Ivanov before assuring one another that the boy was indeed inside the apartment. They locked the door with a key that they found inside.

'Give this key to Inspector Fleischaker when he arrives.'

'I'm staying put?' the other StB officer questioned.

'We wouldn't want the boy to go anywhere now, would we?' the other man said.

The Gathering Thread

Jiri's heart raced as he listened to the officer's talk from the other side of Mr. Dolya's apartment door. He quietly found a spare key and quietly, carefully turned the lock. He looked through the peephole and saw the other StB officer who had been left behind to stand guard of the apartment. The officer paced up and down smoking a cigarette.

Jiri heard cats scraping at the window. As many as four, oh no wait, five cats lined up with a desperate need to come inside. He had forgotten about the smell which still lingered from the small bedroom. It didn't matter now. Nothing did. Jiri was running on adrenaline, and even as he watched through the peephole, his thoughts raced. Visions of what might have happened to his father and knowing that his mother had been taken away from him, so fast ... so fast ... simply didn't make any sense.

Pavel Fleischaker arrived at the Ivanov apartment red--faced and anxious. Accompanying him were four more StB agents, all with military duffel bags.

'Where's the boy?' Pavel boomed.

The StB agent who guarded the apartment door sniffed the air. The distinct odour and the mark left on Pavel's frock jacket were both worthy of comment. 'What's with the gasoline smell? Have you been sniffing toxic substances again?' the agent snickered forcefully. It was a lame joke. He had no idea how close to the mark he was.

'No.' Pavel replied with a straight face. 'Is Patricia Ivanov still inside?'

'On her way to Ústavní 91. She flipped out at the news; left kicking and screaming, just like you said.'

Jiri listened and took a mental note. Ústavní 91 ... although he had no idea what it was, he knew it was important.

Pavel tried the door to the Ivanov apartment. It was locked.

'Where's Jiri?'

'He's in there!' the agent on guard said as he dangled the Ivanov apartment key on a string from his smallest finger. Pavel took the key and the StB on guard asked, 'So you were the one who found him dead?'

Pavel waited beside the door. He swung the keys around his finger. Jiri watched as he looked down the corridor. It was as if he was waiting for something ... or someone.

'I found him lying dead on the road. He shot himself. Personally I feel betrayed ...' Pavel continued. 'The most horrific thing I have ever seen. Nikolai burnt the Killian farmhouse to the ground, with Reznik still inside, and his family were found hanging. Butchered.' Pavel explained, 'We found Nikolai's car not far down the road. Dax Shandling's body, dismembered. A horribly savage scene.'

'Good lord.'

The GATHERING Thread

'You'll hear all about it in the official report.'

Upon hearing Pavel's conversation, Jiri's heart sank into his stomach. He felt sick. He shook his head and mouthed a string of endless silent questions and emphatic denials.

Pavel unlocked the door and called in.

'Jiri. It's the police. We're here to take care of you Jiri. We're going to see to it that you are safe. Don't be alarmed.' He laughed back at one of the men, and whispered, 'That little prick won't know what hit him.'

All four agents piled into the apartment after Pavel. The door was left wide open for all to see. Jiri opened the apartment door ajar, just enough so he could see and hear what they were up to.

Whatever they were doing in the apartment, they weren't treating it with any sense of respect.

THUD, SMACK, SLAP, FLUMP, CLATTER: There seemed to be an urgency to their actions. They pulled over bookcases, and from what Jiri could see, they were searching for specific items.

Pavel came thundering back out of the apartment. Jiri pulled Mr. Dolya's door closed, fast. He quietly turned the key, locked the door and took to the peephole once more.

Pavel looked up and down the corridor – obviously at a loss as to where Jiri was hiding.

'C'mon Jiri ... I don't have time for games. This is serious.' He rapped his fists against the front door and cursed with words that even Jiri didn't know. Jiri held his breath as Pavel turned his back, but then, slowly, Pavel turned around and looked straight at Mr. Dolya's door. His eyes were staring right into the peephole, right at Jiri.

Pavel moved forward until the view of the spy hole was obscured into darkness.

Outside Mr. Dolya's apartment, Pavel tried the handle of the apartment door. The very fact that it was locked should have been enough for him to realise there was nothing for him there. Something brewed behind his grease-lathered hands that led him to believe otherwise. He stood back and gave the door a hefty kick with his boot. After noticing the door had sustained minor damage, he went in with a second boot to the door and then followed that with a full shoulder barge that forced the door clear off its hinges.

The first thing that caught his eye was the window that had been left wide open. The freezing cold air made the apartment feel like an icebox. Three or four cats had already made their way inside, all by habit…

By ritual.

They stopped where they either stood or sat and looked at Pavel with wide, unflinching eyes — as though he was the one who had no right to be there. As Pavel advanced towards the window, the chorus of hissing, spitting, and growls filled the room. Behind him, more cats poured in. They too took a stance against him.

#

Minutes later, Pavel was in the backseat of his Skoda 1102 with the fellow StB officer at the wheel. Pavel dabbed a cloth against his cheek where the deepest of the scratches had gone beyond the drawing blood. His hands were marred with sporadic scratch marks — likely accounting for his momentary struggle trying to be sure that Jiri wasn't somewhere hiding in Mr. Dolya's apartment. Pavel had put up quite a fight, but ultimately, he gave in. It took a lot for him to take the back seat of his own car, and upon giving the keys to the StB officer in charge of driving, he warned,

'You dare put a scratch on this classic and I'll beat you unrecognisable.'

The StB officer laughed it off this time. It was safe to say Pavel wasn't in the mood to follow through on any idle threats, even if they were only for show. Some people took it seriously, and the others, like those who knew him best, took it how it was: an attempt at dark humour to lighten an already awkward situation.

'Pavel.' the StB officer noted, 'your front light isn't working. If I clip the curb and ruin your trims, I'm not taking the blame.'

'The car's fine. Will get it fixed.' Pavel answered. 'Just drive.'

'Is Jiri going to be okay on his own?'

'I'm not worried about the boy.' Pavel said. 'He's

bound to go visit his mother. I'll get him then. She's all he's got. I will have to be patient.'

'What do you mean patient?' the StB officer asked. 'What are you going to do with the boy?'

Pavel gave the StB a glaring look that meant more to himself than to the officer. The answer to that question was far too telling. The reasoning itself was brooding behind subconscious thoughts.

The StB officer carried on driving and didn't think anything more of Jiri. He did however want to know about Nikolai. Everybody did.

'I can't believe it was Nikolai who engineered all the murders.' he said. 'We've all known him since before the war. Just doesn't add up.'

'You'll see in the coming months when the crime wave dips.' Pavel mumbled to himself as he sucked on his hand that stung and ached from the feline assault.

'I still don't believe it.' the StB officer said. 'I mean there's plenty of reason, and we've had our suspicions about Nikolai's abilities to hone in so quickly to details ... I hope we're not missing something. What if you're wrong and it's—'

'Believe it!' Pavel interrupted. 'Believe it. It's the only explanation. The pieces fit.'

'Oh I believe it, but I'm not the judge. I suppose it's just hard to wrap my head around.'

Pavel felt his temper begin to flare. He looked at the driver as though he was some kind of an idiot. It didn't matter either way whether he could get his head around it. Some of the most incredible events in history still baffle us, so why should it matter for this situation with Nikolai?

If this officer needed so much convincing, Pavel knew it was not going to be easy to persuade those who were otherwise detached from any personal experience, or feelings.

14

ÚSTAVNÍ 91 SANITARIUM

THREE DAYS LATER – DAWN

Jiri and Karel scrambled across the Northern quarter and headed into areas of Prague where neither of them had ever been. After hearing what Jiri had gone through, Karel was convinced that his good friend and fellow truant needed help.

Karel was a wealth of information and also embellishment. Jiri explained that his mother had been taken away and that his father was not coming home. He spared Karel the details of what Pavel had uttered in the corridor, for he himself did not believe that his own father was responsible for any wrongdoing. It didn't surprise Jiri at all that Pavel wanted people to think it was Nikolai. Jiri had always thought there was something wrong with Pavel, from his attitude and behaviour. It cut deeply to think he was free to make up whatever he wanted, and nobody, not Jiri nor his mother, and certainly not his father, could say or do anything to prevent him from spreading the lies.

#

Days before when Jiri had explained to Karel that his mother had been taken away on a stretcher, Karel was quick off the mark to say that she was going to be thrown in an asylum.

'That's where mad people go.' Karel noted. Jiri was quick to refute that assessment.

'She's not mad.' Jiri said without any annoyance. Karel said shitty things about people all the time, and didn't know any better. Jiri then sweetened the pot. 'She knows things ...'

'What kind of things?' Karel asked with hungry curiosity.

'I have to find her.' Jiri was not in the mood to hide behind any bravado, nor did he care to act tough in front of his friend anymore. Tears were in his eyes. Karel knew what that meant. Something was hurting.

'I know where she is.' Karel said with the confidence of a know-it-all. Once they figure out how to sneak into the local library without being seen, they found the maps, reference books and information they needed to pinpoint the address that lit a thousand gas lamps above Jiri's little head.

'Ústavní 91, San-ahhhh.' Jiri stumbled on the difficult word and then slapped his hand on the book. 'I heard about that. That's what he said … that's where they took my mother.'

#

Here they both were, amongst the trees in the early hours of the morning. They stared across at the most foreboding building that they'd ever seen. There was a main road between them and the black wrought-iron fence that stretched around a vast area before them. Behind the fence, there seemed to be many grand buildings.

'How are we going to find her? It's massive.' Jiri asked.

Karel was quiet. He didn't want to show Jiri that he'd lost his nerve all of a sudden. The place didn't look welcoming. The building didn't look to be fun. Even though the prospect of seeing crazy people in all states of madness did excite him, it also terrified him.

For sure, he'd lost his nerve. He pushed Jiri forward, urging him to go on ahead.

'I'll stand guard here. You go on!'

Jiri turned, forcing against the resistance of Karel's hands as they pushed.

'I'm not going in there alone.'

Karel pushed again. 'Go on. I helped you this far. I'll wait here for you.'

Jiri moved on ahead. He had waited long enough for this. He hollered back.

'How do I get over the gate?'

'Just like I showed you before, you *dum-dum*, use your coat!'

Jiri took his coat off. The winter chill raced through to his skin with seconds.

'Hey Jiri!' Karel yelled out and as Jiri turned, Karel made a face of disfigurement. He arched his body and twisted his arms in an obscene manner. 'Don't catch the crazy. Don't catch the crazy!'

Jiri frowned and threw his hands up in an vulgar gesture of "taking somebody's nose" to which Karel laughed and returned the gesture.

Jiri felt inside his jacket and carefully tucked his father's mysterious notebook into the stretchy waistband of his trousers. He threw his jacket over the fence, and managed to catch the sleeve on two of the sharp prongs. He pulled his jacket back, tearing the arm. After a hefty sigh he made a second attempt. This time he managed to throw the jacket clear over the prongs. Behind him, car lights loomed in from the main road, and he hastily pulled himself up and then — after a moment of hesitating — made his descent onto the other side of the fence. He tugged at his jacket but it wouldn't return to him without a fight. Having left his jacket behind, he checked the notebook was still safe in his trouser waistband and crept across to the first building in what was a field of white buildings.

Up until this point, Jiri had only seeing his

mother in mind. Now that he was close, he wondered what he would do if he found her. If they both managed to get out together, where would they go? His mother had nobody, and there was no going back home. Days after his mother had been taken, Jiri watched the apartment block from a safe distance. Mr. Dolya never came back – and that alone would be left open as something of an unsolved mystery.

All the while, Jiri would be on the run, fearing the wrath of Pavel Fleischaker. Pavel had campaigned hard to convince everybody in the high police that his father had in fact been Tobe Healy all along, and for some reason, they all bought it. With no Nikolai alive to defend himself, it was the easy route to solving the case.

In time, once the killings started again, Pavel's story would crumble and perhaps then Jiri and his mother would be able to clear Nikolai's name and regain their protection.

Or maybe that was just a dream ...

Whatever the case, they had to stay out of sight. Jiri couldn't let himself get taken by anybody, not by Tobe or by Pavel who may very well be acting as Mr. Healy's right hand man. It was not a coincidence that Pavel framed Nikolai when on the day after his death, he himself was reeking of petrol. Why Tobe couldn't do the work himself was the biggest mystery of them all.

Unless ...

Unless ...

What if there really was no Tobe Healy?

The book Jiri held tight in his hand was the only thing left of his father's life, as both an investigator, and as his protector. What it would mean to him, he did not know.

He crept over to the buildings, avoided windows and doors, and made sure to take cover in whatever growth was available to him.

Jiri felt a sensation from inside his jacket. He stopped behind another tree and opened the book. As before, in his apartment, he opened the book to a blank page. He waited a few breaths until words began to form:

Warmer.

Jiri was both baffled and amazed. Something or someone was guiding him, and just like the message that his mother projected onto the page one time before in their apartment, he guessed that it could only be her again. She knew he was there, and he was getting closer.

Jiri placed the book into his jacket and carried on to wherever the warm feeling led him. He soon found a fenced-off area with gardens that sprawled across the hillside, many with pathways which led to more single-storey buildings. He finally came to a main road; the circuit road that ran the entire perimeter of the sanatorium grounds. The road led all the way around, spurring off to a large set of gates where cars were parked. He hurried along past a taller building that appeared well-lit with offices, and thereafter, more three-storey buildings with bars on their windows, most likely keeping those inside from getting out.

Jiri crept along that building with his head down low, until he felt a tap from one of the barred windows. The tap came from inside.

'Mother?' he thought as he raced back to the window. He grabbed hold of the bars and lifted himself off the ground so he could look in. Suddenly a face appeared looking back at him. It was a woman with tangled hair, no teeth, and bloodshot eyes. She appeared to moan and wail. Upon seeing Jiri she stared at him and the wailing became a scream.

Definitely not Mother.

Jiri was terrified and dropped instantly to the ground. He sat on the ground below the crazy old lady's window and opened the notebook for guidance.

There were no words to be found.

He carried on along the side of the building, as he was before the scary lady got his attention, and the book felt warm again.

Soon enough there was another tap on a window. It was a very specific tap which Jiri recognised to be the last line of Pop Goes the

Weasel. A sign for sure. He walked along and found a hand pressed against a window. Behind the hand was the solemn face of Patricia, his mother.

Jiri's hand went up through the bars and touched the glass. His hand met with hers and she tried, oh boy did she try, to smile for him.

'Can I come in.' Jiri said as loud as he felt he could talk.

Patricia shook her head. A tear rose and fell from her ducts. Her eyes swelled and she wiped her streaming nose.

'How can I see you ...?' Jiri asked.

Patricia lowered her head. The separation hit them both in a wave of hopelessness, and as the feeling crashed, Jiri started to cry. Seeing his mother being carried away deep inside grief sealed his breath.

Nikolai's notebook was the only connection that he would have with his mother, for now. He'd never felt so alone.

The notebook within his jacket began to warm up again.

He got his answer. He opened it and saw, there on the first page:

Your father is still the protector. He is still with us.

The book suddenly felt very warm in his hand; beyond that of tolerable comfort. Jiri looked down at his hand; he thought he could see an aura emanating from his palms. The emanation faded, or perhaps he'd never seen one to begin with. Perhaps his eyes were playing tricks, and the thermal sense was also as easily written off as being that of wishful thinking. Still, Jiri had the feeling that book was demanding his attention.

A noise.

The sound of feet forced Jiri to duck down, out of sight of the window and quietly, with controlled excitement he turned the page of the notebook. Jiri gasped! Suddenly every page was suddenly full of his father's hand-written scrawls — detailing chronological accounts that spanned decades. Words, sketches, forms and structures, with circles swarming about, connecting the dots or scribbling out false leads. Some thick-etched arrows pointed to words that were heavily underlined. Several words caught his eye: "killings" and "blood-soaked" among many. All of a sudden the words on the page, the diagrams, and hand-drawn maps began to fade before his eyes. He leafed through the book as fast as he could, but his ability to read the fading words became a losing battle. Jiri flipped back to the first few pages to find them already blank.

Seeing his father's writings, albeit briefly, gave him very little comfort. Even if it was meant to give Jiri something to hang his hopes onto, it did nothing to help him find his way to his mother. He wondered what Nikolai would have done if he were here. He'd be so adamant that he was going to see Patricia that he would just walk right in that building and demand that somebody open the door. There really wasn't any other way of doing it.

Perhaps that's what Jiri should do. Just go in and demand to see his mother. Breaking in always set the wheels in motion for the possibility of getting caught. Getting caught tarnished the Ivanov name. So perhaps it was time for a change of pace. Besides, it didn't hurt to try and do things right: like any regular kid who seriously missed his mother should.

15

ÚSTAVNÍ 91 SANITARIUM

LOT#71 – MOMENTS LATER

Jiri did what he thought was right. He walked away from his mother's window and walked right around to the main doors. He tried them, and they opened. As he stepped in he counted the pairs of eyes that looked at him. Four pairs, three women, one man. One was a cleaner who was filling up her bucket at a sink before setting it down on a wheeled contraption that allowed her to speed up her floor cleaning duties. The other two women sat, one at a typewriter, the other one reading. The man was the first to stand. He had a telephone receiver.. He quietly whispered into the mouthpiece and hung up the phone.

'Excuse me.' Jiri started. 'I'm here to visit my mother.'

The cleaner stopped wringing out her mop to listen. The woman with the book stood and started to advance to Jiri.

'Where on earth did you come from?'

'Excuse me, son, but what do you think you're doing?' the male doctor said.

'I'm here to see my mother.' Jiri spoke his truth with an air of absolutes as if stating that grass was green and the sky was blue.

The woman at the typewriter turned, 'This facility does not allow visitors.' She then gestured to the man and said in a hushed tone 'You should call the officer on duty to escort him off the premises.'

The woman who was reading approached Jiri, softly, 'I'm afraid you're going to have to take a seat.' She pointed to a chair behind a vacant desk.

'Who exactly are you here to visit, *son*?' the male doctor said. Jiri didn't like to hear that term "son" used by a stranger and chose to ignore him. He instead approached the woman.

'Excuse me. I mean no harm. My mother is here and I haven't seen her since she was brought here. I know I'm probably going to be taken away, but I need to speak to my mother. I just need a minute.'

'Are you Jiri Ivanov?' the woman behind the typewriter said, now holding a letter that had been placed on the desk by the StB officer on duty.

Jiri nodded. To lie now would not have gotten

him anywhere.

The two women and the doctor began to talk out of Jiri's immediate earshot. The cleaner with the mop gave Jiri a sympathetic smile before heading off, through a pair of double doors and down the corridor to where patients were being held, or kept, or stored.

The doors swung closed. Jiri thought about his options. The cleaner did not have any keys however. Jiri was smart enough to realise that if he ran down to his mother's room he would be dragged and escorted back within two shakes of a fox's tail. He would then leave the complex without anything gained from the venture.

The trio broke away from their conversation; the doctor went back to the phone to ring in their agreed plan. It was not uncommon for children to want to see family members, especially if they were left to their own devices, with a less than structured or happy life back at home. But very few would get so far as to locate the actual building where said family members were being treated. There was no protocol for this.

It was the friendlier woman who approached Jiri once again. The plan agreed that she already held the boy's attention.

'You realise that you are supposed to be under the care and guard of an assigned StB officer. One that worked with your father. Now I've heard enough to know that you've suffered, but we really don't think that you should see your mother while everything is so... fresh.'

Jiri said nothing. He thought as much and had started to regret not climbing up the drainpipe and tunnelling his way to his mother's room, somehow. He looked away.

The woman behind the typewriter spoke to the man who was hanging on at the other side of the phone, waiting for a connection.

'Is she dangerous?' the woman said, levelling to her softer side as she looked at Jiri who had taken rejection so quietly and without resistance.

'Who? The mother? No, I don't think so. We have it on good authority that she was possibly another one of Nikolai's victims. Possibly, he kept her at their family home against her will. He may be responsible for her state of mind.'

Jiri listened to the conversation. It was not hard to miss as the room's acoustics were nothing if not "projecting" of any noise. He leaned in to talk with the lady. 'Please, my father is not a bad man. My mother is not sick because of him either. They brought me up to recognise evil and to ensure that I stood for the good in all people. My father is ...' Jiri stopped. He still didn't know if his father was truly dead or not. His honesty was the one thing that had gotten him there thus far and so, he kept it going. 'I don't know if he is dead. My mother seems to think so. I need her. She needs me.'

The sympathetic woman was clearly touched by Jiri's plea. The woman behind the typewriter was less enthused and the man on the phone received his orders directly from the man in charge, and wasn't in the mood to listen to anything but his orders. He did however look at Jiri whenever he wasn't speaking, and then after that, he would turn away so that he wasn't heard.

'We need our mothers, Jiri, but your situation is a little different.' the sympathetic woman said.

The doctor hung up his phone once more.

'Jiri, you're in luck. Your mother will be having a little recreation with the other patients at eight o'clock this morning. If you would just wait there until then, I will escort you personally to the recreation garden and you can have a special, one-off, supervised visit. But only for ten minutes. I trust you find that acceptable?'

Jiri looked up at the clock. There still half an hour until eight o'clock, and from what it looked like, the doctor was checking something over with the man at the other end of the phone that didn't feel right.

The sympathetic woman looked back at them, almost assuaging Jiri's concerns that something didn't seem quite right. The woman at the typewriter felt the need to pass another comment.

'Gwyn, leave the boy in peace and come finish these reports.'

'I was actually on break!' Gwyn replied with a snap in her tongue. She turned back to Jiri and smiled. 'It's going to be okay, Jiri. It's going to work out.'

She returned to her desk, picked up her book

but then was chastised by the woman behind the typewriter.

'Your break's over.'

Gwyn snapped the book shut. The doctor reached for his beverage and commented that it was cold.

'This tea is old. Where's Ingrid?' he said.

The woman at the typewriter sighed. 'She's finishing the floors and then she's on transportation duty. She's busy enough. Go get your own tea.'

The doctor then looked over at the seat where Jiri sat. The chair was empty.

'Hey, where did he go?' he said, jumping out of his chair. He ran to the doors and took a look outside. He wasn't the type to give chase. It was too early in the morning for that. 'Suppose I better make another phone call.'

#

Jiri ran back, past his mother's window to the far end of the building. He looked behind him to see if anybody was deft enough to catch up. When he saw that nobody had bothered, he slowed down. He reached the end and started to think once again about how Karel would have handled this. At the rear of the building he found a single exit, but there was no handle. A loose breeze block was set against the wall, which often meant that it was one of those doors that only ever opened from the inside. The block would be used as a wedge to prevent anybody from getting locked out. That was no use to Jiri in this instance. He wanted to get in, but he kept the door's quirk in mind.

Nearby drains reeked of sewage and filth. He looked up and examined the thick drainpipes that were made of a mixture of light grade PVC and clay. Leaks had obviously been patched up, making it unsafe to climb. Even Jiri wasn't that stupid, having already slipped halfway down one of the pipes in his own building. In that instance he had had no choice. Pavel was after him. Jiri was lucky to have been so close to the ground when he slipped. He looked up and thought better of it. He simply didn't know what he would have done had he gotten up there.

Suddenly the back door opened. Jiri watched as the cleaner struggled to keep the door open with her steel bucket and mop both in hand. Jiri was startled enough to fall to the ground. He scrambled back. The cleaner put the bucket down against the wall and moved toward Jiri.

'I'm sorry. I didn't see you there,' the cleaner began.

Jiri scrambled back and was ready to run. He looked at the open door however, and saw his chance … but then, as the cleaner leaned down to extend a hand, the door closed and the cleaner turned around and cursed.

'Beitsim!' the cleaner cursed.

'I'm sorry. I didn't mean to.' Jiri found his feet and started to walk away.

'It's okay. I do it all the time.' The cleaner returned to Jiri with a calm voice. 'You're Jiri, aren't you?'

Jiri stopped. He sniffed for an opportunity. He was out in the open and fast on his feet. There was no reason not to engage in a conversation if it meant getting close to his mother. This cleaner knew who he was.

'I wanted to see my mother. But I don't think I'm allowed.'

The cleaner stayed where she was and projected her voice to Jiri, knowing that he was far too easy to scare away.

'No. You haven't a chance in hell. I'm Ingrid by the way.' She extended a hand. Jiri didn't dare come any closer. Ingrid indicated her hands, brushing her palms. 'Don't worry. They're quite clean.'

'How do you know my name?'

'Lucky guess. Spied a telegram on the desk several days ago telling us that if a young boy of ten turned up, matching your description, answering to the name of Jiri Ivanov, well,' she chuckled, 'we had to call you in.'

'Call me in?' Jiri reiterated.

'Yeah, to the StB. I have to say, you look dangerous.' She laughed again. 'Your mother has been through quite the drama it seems. A life of chaos. But I don't see how being dragged away from her son is considered to be healthy, or helpful.' She clicked and shrugged. 'But what do I know.'

'I don't know why they took her way. I can take care of her.'

'It's a bad situation to be in.' Ingrid sat down against the wall, moving the brick out of the way. Jiri recognised her stance and walked a little closer to her to talk. 'You seem the type to do okay on your own. You want to take care of her yourself?'

'Yes.' Jiri nodded. 'At eight, she's going to be in the garden for recre–'

'They're lying to you. Oh, but not about the recreation. That always happens at eight. Your mother won't be joining them.'

Jiri was silent.

'It's okay. She's just being moved to another building. She's getting her own room with her own guard until the situation with your father is resolved. I feel very sorry for you…'

'I don't know what happened to my father.' Jiri said, now with tears streaming down his cheeks.

'Don't cry.' Ingrid said sternly, shaking her head. She looked away. 'You'll ruin me for the rest of the day if you cry.'

Jiri couldn't help it, he sat on the grass and held his head down in despair.

'Oh stop it!' Ingrid snapped. 'Do you want to see your mother like that?'

'I can't see her. They won't let me.'

'At eight o'clock, your mother is going to be transported by car to her new building. They do it at eight so that it counts as her recreation.

The Gathering Thread

Apparently walking to and from a car is enough to be classed as exercise. If that's right then I'm an athlete.' Ingrid laughed at her own joke.

Jiri laughed too. It was probably the first time he'd laughed in ... oh, he had no idea.

'You sound like my mother.' Jiri said.

'If I were in your shoes ... ' Ingrid thought for a moment. She tapped her pocket and pulled out a cigarette. She struck a match and took a few drags before continuing. 'I have been in your shoes. I lost my entire family during the war. Brothers, sisters, mother, and father ... but I hid from those German bastards ... Excuse my language. I didn't say goodbye, Jiri, and who'd have thought that years after beating the fascists at their game that we'd be here again, seeing children pulled away from their parents, not because of where they are from, but because of who they are.'

'How can I see my mother if she's going to be taken away in a car? I don't understand.'

'Well, your mother will be driven by me.'

'You're just a cleaner?' Jiri smirked.

'How very dare.' Ingrid said with a tut. She placed the cigarette in her mouth and reached for her pocket and pulled out a set of keys. 'I've worked here for seventeen years. I get to do all the jobs nobody can be bothered to do.' She replaced the keys and removed her cigarette. 'How do you think I managed to survive the war?'

'Which car?'

'The tanned Skoda with the grill divide. You

won't miss it. I'll let you into a secret: I leave it unlocked when it's not in use. That way I remember to lock it when I transport patients to and from the infirmary, or wherever it is they're heading.' She took a breath. A drag of smoke that was held in her lungs made her voice sound restrained. 'Now I don't want to see you. I don't want you to announce yourself. Get yourself hidden in the foot well of the back seat. I'm not even going to tell your mother that you're there.' She exhaled. 'Between you and me and your mother, we never had this conversation. Is that clear?'

'Yes.' Jiri beamed. It was enough. He looked around for the car in question and was ready to head that way now. He knew eight o'clock was looming fast. He turned to thank Ingrid, but the door beside her started to open.

Jiri gasped. Ingrid stood in a panicked fluster. It was Gwyn. As the door opened wide, she looked about but didn't see anything beyond Ingrid, her mop, and the smoke she had clung between her teeth.

Jiri had gone.

'Ingrid. It's nearly eight.' Gwyn announced with a condescending tone.

'I know. The door closed on me again.' She pushed the brick against the now-open door and started to empty her bucket and squeeze out her mop. 'I thought I'd sneak in a smoke before I go on car duty.'

Gwyn looked across the grounds once more. 'Did you see the boy?'

'The boy?'

'Yes, the boy who was waiting in with us.'

'No. He's probably long gone. You don't exactly have any candy to offer children, so why would he stay.'

'Never mind.' Gwyn checked if the brick was in place to keep the door from closing again. 'Don't be late. Pavel Fleischaker will be receiving Patricia at the other end. You know what the StB are like about punctuality.'

'I know.' Ingrid said. 'They're a real drag.' She sucked the life out of the last bit of her cigarette before throwing to the ground. She stubbed it out, collected her mop and bucket, and headed back in, kicking the brick out of its place.

The door closed.

#

Jiri opened the back door of the only car that had the grill divide that protected the driver from the back seat reserved for the insane. He quietly hid on the floor directly behind the passenger seat. He assumed that his mother would get in the car on the side nearest to the building. He waited for what felt like forever until he heard movement outside the window.

In that moment, he had second thoughts. What if this was just another trap; in an endless run of traps upon traps, where running became the only constant that kept him one step ahead of getting caught?

Jiri lost his nerve. He felt a sensation in his pocket. A burning that came from the notebook. Was it a warning? He daren't reach in now. He had to think on his feet. On his knees he looked out of the window. His breath had already started to fog up the glass. As he quickly wiped at the window, he noticed somebody moving in the blur of condensation. Sure enough, he saw his mother approaching — wearing all white — with a soft smile on her face. It was as if she knew already that Jiri was waiting for her.

Ingrid was there with her, just as she said she would be. She wore a blue jacket now and a soft flat cap giving her the look of an official driver. She reached for the passenger seat and allowed Patricia the freedom to climb in of her own volition. Patricia needed no further direction. She ducked under the doorframe and sat straight up, face forward. A lock turned from the outside securing the door. Patricia smiled down at Jiri and said,

'Jiri. I knew you were there. I could feel it. Did you feel it burning …'

Jiri remembered the book, and he smiled and nodded. He was all ready to jump up and into her arms. He heard Ingrid arrive on the driver's side and she too found her seat. As Jiri rose to his knees, Ingrid flipped her driver's mirror to catch his eyes.

'Jiri!' Ingrid said with a stern voice. 'You must

not be seen from the window. Stay down!'

The car pulled out of its parking place and began slowly, extremely slowly down the road.

Patricia lay her head down onto the seat so that she could hold Jiri with discretion. There were no words needed in that moment as Jiri's smaller hands gripped her with all his might. She kissed his head and smelt his hair.

'I'm so sorry Jiri. So sorry.' She repeated over and over.

Ingrid faced forward as her two passengers shared their private moment. Time was shorter than ever before.

'Mother, are you coming home?' Jiri asked the question, even though the absence of home didn't register in his mind. Home was a ransacked mess that didn't even look like an apartment where a family could live. The apartment was no different from one of his father's crime scenes. Still, no matter their reality, wherever they ended up, his mother was the only person right now who could make anywhere a home.

'Things have changed, Jiri. I have to stay here.'

Jiri's heart sunk to a new depth. He looked into her eyes. 'I don't want leave you here. I need you! Father needs you too!'

Again Jiri was reaching to the unknown or at least that which remained unconfirmed. Even though the two policemen did arrive and tell his mother that Nikolai's life had been taken, those words were meaningless without any further proof. Indeed, until he saw a body, his father was still out there working, as always. Until there was a reason to stop thinking he was alive, Nikolai was still coming home and his mother couldn't be there when he did if she remained in this hellhole.

'I cannot go back, Jiri. It's not safe for me anymore. In a way, I have always known he would catch up with us. I pictured it differently.'

Jiri pleaded with the only thing that he had to bargain. He started to cry. Things were sinking in slowly.

'I need you.'

'I need you too, my sweet boy.' Patricia had a resigned look in her eyes. 'But for now, neither of us are safe in the world as long as ... as long as he is looking for us, there is no home.'

'The apartment has already been searched. I didn't like seeing that.' Jiri said. 'They took things.'

'Pavel would have turned our place upside down. Where have you been staying?'

'Mr. Dolya's. It smells funny but Pavel doesn't like the cats. They don't like him either. Not at all.'

Patricia let out a little smile but then returned to business. She knew the car journey through the complex wasn't going to last.

'You can't stay here in Prague. I need you to find something for me, in the apartment. Did they take the curtains?'

'The curtains?'

'Yes, did they take the curtains?'

'They ripped them to shreds.'

'But did they leave the rail? The thick oak rail where the curtains hung?'

'No. I think that's still up there. I see the rings.'

'Unscrew the right end. Dig deep. Inside there will be a letter.'

'A letter?'

'Two actually. One for you, and one for my sister.'

'Your sister?' Jiri asked puzzled.

'Yes, but I don't want to talk about it here. You have to promise me that whatever you read in that letter, the letter to you, that you must do as I say. Please. You have to promise me.'

'What do you want me to do?'

'Just read the letter and remember, you're never going to be safe as long as you are here in Prague.'

The car pulled into a spot and Ingrid tapped on the steering wheel.

'Patricia. We're here.' Ingrid grunted, 'and so is Inspector Fleischaker. Oh the joys. You better say your goodbyes, Jiri. Hurry now.'

Jiri froze and Patricia pushed him down as far as she could.

'Jiri, stay down.' She said with limited lip movement. Pavel moved to the driver window and Ingrid struggled to wind it down to talk. Only an inch or so was enough.

'Inspector.' Ingrid smiled.

'What took you so long? You left at eight. Does it take twenty minutes to get around the complex?'

Ingrid smiled even more. 'Twenty minutes is

how long the patient has for recreation. I was making sure Patricia here got a little scenery. A little daylight and fresh air. You don't have to thank me.'

Pavel passed a note through the gap in the window.

'You better send this back to the staff at LOT#71. Confidential.'

Ingrid took the telegram and then handed Pavel the key to the door. He moved from the window and went to open the door. He took a long look inside before he requested Patricia step out.

Patricia spat a huge wad on Pavel's winter coat. He looked away and attempted to contain himself from anger.

'I just needed to get that out of my system. Better out than in …' Patricia said, in complete control of herself. She slowly stepped out and straight away, she turned, faced the car and put her hands behind her back. 'Because of that, you must cuff me. Save further embarrassment to your dry cleaning inspection.'

Pavel did just that. He cuffed her and leaned into her, reasserting his complete control over her.

'One down. Two to go.' he said to her before he led her away. He held her at the back of the neck, and made sure she didn't attempt anything else out of the ordinary. They arrived at the doors, which were opened by another man in a raincoat.

Ingrid watched as they went inside, as did Jiri whose heart split into more pieces than he could ever manage to find or put back together.

Ingrid read the telegram. She was aghast at what it said.

'Well, you're not going to believe this, Jiri. You just got caught.'

Jiri was already too upset. His tear-soaked eyes darted left and right. He scrambled but felt Ingrid tap her fingers on the telegram.

'Now don't worry, Jiri. You're free to go, but please let me read this note before you run: I don't think this has anything to do with you. The telegram says that Jiri was found and picked up by a passing VB officer, just outside the institute on the main road. Now if you think about it, I'm sure...' she turned. The back seat was empty. The foot well of the backseat was empty and the far side rear passenger door was wide open.

Ingrid smiled. 'You're welcome, Jiri. Safe travels.'

#

Pavel ensured that Patricia was locked away. His eyes tightened with the glimmer of success mixed in with a feeling of guilt. As Patricia sat on the chair looking as lost as she had ever been, he walked away.

Outside the building he received word that the car that had picked up a boy on the main road was arriving at the main gates. Pavel was pleased, for he knew he had done his duty to the one who lurked in the shadows of every corner of his life. He would owe nothing more to the one who wanted Jiri under his control. The voices in Pavel's head had pulled him apart like a fattened goose these last few days; insisting and intending on more horrors had these events not played out in their favour.

Patricia was one of three, but Jiri was the key. Two down …

Healy …That's right, Pavel thought. I have them both.

The car arrived and Pavel couldn't wait to get his hands on the car door. He knew that Jiri would be a very slippery creature. For sure, Pavel had his work cut out for him.

I would have to put him away. Lock him up. Pavel thought. He saw the back of the boy's head in the unmarked police car, but the feeling behind his eyes were already one step ahead of him.

The feeling of doubt was confirmed as he opened the car door. The boy who sat on the back seat was not Jiri Ivanov.

'What … I thought you said.'

The uniformed officer stepped out and straightaway went to collect the boy from the backseat. As the boy stepped out of the car, he looked up at Pavel with eyes of regret.

It was Karel.

'Who are you?' Pavel boomed.

'Karel. My name is Karel Hamm. I didn't mean

to skip school! Please.' He trembled. 'I'm sorry. Please don't tell my father!'

Pavel was no longer listening. He felt as though his world was spinning. Jiri wasn't here.

Jiri was not here at all.

His key ... his freedom, was still unclaimed.

Insert chapter ten text here. Insert chapter ten text here. Insert chapter ten text here. Insert chapter ten text here.

16

THE IVANOV APARTMENT

LATER THAT AFTERNOON

Jiri approached the place he once called home with a sense of trepidation. Even though there was no sign of Pavel's car, Jiri had a feeling he was never going to be too far away.

The door to the Ivanov apartment was chaired off. The very idea that Pavel would take one of their own dining room chairs and place it out in the corridor played on Jiri in two ways. First, it reminded him of the armchair that had growled at him beforehand. Whoever had the power to make inanimate objects come alive in order to put the living fear into the world was not likely to stop anytime soon. As far as Jiri was concerned, chairs were handled like fire. Secondly: Nothing in their apartment – or what was left anyway – was their property anymore. Nothing would be inherited through the family line. Nothing would be held with the same reverence as it had when the Ivanov lived within those four walls, together, as a family.

Jiri stood at the chair and reached out his hand slowly. He closed his eyes until his hand made contact with the wood. It felt as ordinary as a chair should. He slid the chair out of the way and with his own key, he opened the door.

The main hallway was cold and still. The carpet runner was no longer there, nor any of the other rugs that once grounded everything and gave the place exuberance and instant warmth. There were smashed lamps, smashed furniture, drawers scattered, shelving skewed, and books torn from their hardback covers. Pavel and the other police officers had searched every post, platform, and pillar —not that the apartment was particularly palatial to begin with.

To Jiri's surprise, they had not touched the curtain rail that his mother told him to check. It was strange to think that they had gone to such trouble to break open clocks, rip apart cushions and pillows, cut into the couches and chairs, smash mirrors, and split the hem of curtains, but never once did they look up and think that the curtain rail could be the perfect hiding place.

He would have used one of the dining room chairs to stand up on to so he could reach the rail, but all but one had been destroyed, piled in the middle of the main living space. Instead, he picked up his father's solid wood bureau drawer and tipped it on its side.

He reached up to the ornately carved rail end and began to turn it anticlockwise in order to loosen it. Once he had unscrewed it, he tried to peer into the hollow rail but couldn't see anything.

Dig deep.

That's what his mother had said to him. He stuck his youthful fingers into the hollow of the rail, but his fingers did not settle on anything specific.

He hopped down and went for his mother's shoehorn, but it was too thick to stick down the rail. It wasn't the right angle to dig deep, and so he pushed the rail up until it lifted out of its curved wall mount. The drawer beneath his feet rocked as he lifted it around until it was loose. Suddenly he was face level with the sloped hollow of the curtain rail. Something cylindrical ran down and hit him square on the head. He rocked, lost his footing, and collapsed on the floor with a bump. The curtain rail clattered to the ground, then settled on the floor next to him. Jiri stood, brushed himself off and picked up the cylindrical package. It was a piece of copper pipe, no longer than his arm. He felt his forehead where the object had hit him; although it hurt, there was no blood.

He found his mother's blanket and placed it on the ground. He spilled out the contents of the copper pipe onto it with a sense of achievement.

'I found it, mother.' He spoke down into his jacket. Indeed, the notebook was snug and warm within the inside pocket. He pulled it out and saw a message three pages in.

Keep your ears and eyes peeled.

Jiri closed the notebook and ran to the window. The road outside was too busy to recognise anything familiar. People walked up and down the street. Any one of them could be Pavel, Mr. Dolya or dare he say it ... Healy.

He realised that he had to pay attention to the corridor outside the apartment door more than anything. He wished he had the means of creating an early warning system. However, he believed that he was so alert that he would hear a whisker twitch on the snout of a dormouse. He settled on the rug and looked carefully at the secret hoard.

First, he unrolled two letters that were both sealed within envelopes. One envelope carried the number 2, the other, 3.

Jiri unravelled another letter that was not in an envelope with the expectation of finding the number 1, but as he flattened it out in its intended form, he found that it was meant for him.

He held it up to the light of the window and began to read, slowly and carefully.

Dearest Jiri,

I had a feeling the day would come that you would need to find and read this letter. If things have gone the way I've always imagined, and feared, then I doubt you have much time. I'm not going to talk in riddles, cushion the blow, or make light of your situation.

First, you must know that whatever has occurred at the time of reading this, your father and I love you very much. We live for you and believe in only the good. Unfortunately, light cannot function without darkness, and without darkness, how can we recognise the light?

That is important to remember as I explain. I want you to know that whatever you've been through, it is not your fault.

By now you feel like the world is on your shoulders. The truth is, it is. You are the key that can unlock a great many things, and the Venetian Killer known as the "L'assassino di nota" who hunted us down will want to use you to get to the others.

I am a sister, one of three of whom he needs to harness an energy which goes beyond life and death. We are the beginning, the middle, and the end. I am the gatherer of the thread. My sister Angelica is the one who measures its length, and Dee Dee is the one who decides where the thread will be cut. Separate, we are nothing. Together, we are everything. That is what he wants: to bring the trinity together and then...

He will be beyond any god this universe has ever seen. I can't be any more specific about how or why, but that's what I was told when I was about your age.
Three sisters: we were separated at birth. How our parents knew, I have no idea, but there was something that hung over our arrival into the world —as it had been centuries before when we last walked the earth together at the same time — as three.

It is important for you to know: Killing me is the last thing he would want, but it can and will happen somehow. Through time, the Three Threads have always been further apart as distant relations. Every so often, triplets are born and he comes forth and hunts us down.

Do you understand the implications? In simple terms, we three must never meet. The only hope is that we all die in our own time and place, but none of us should seek death, for death will pass the torch to another that will replace us.

Sisters.

They can only ever be sisters who create, measure, and cut the threads of fate. Remember that!

Oh, I hope this makes sense to you. Your father understood it, but wanted to protect me, and let the others find their own means of protection. Most likely by now your father and I have been taken from you. Your life is in danger only if you stay.

This is why you must leave Prague before he gets his hands on you first. You must stay one step ahead ... if not more.

You are the key, and you must warn the other two sisters of his presence, but separately, so they can take matters into their own hands. Never bring them together.
The thread cannot be tied. Not ever.

Trust nobody but your own blood. You will know when you meet them. Their light shines in the same way that you shine. Leave Prague, and head to Boston, England, which is where the second sister was sent (vague, I know. With only the name to go by, it's not going to be easy: remember she was born Angelica Sorrel of Mirano, Veneto, Italia – the small town, not to be confused with the island. Remember that.)

I know you won't want to leave, but I am

telling you, as a mother to her son, whom she loves more than life itself … leave Prague. Do as I ask. Stay in the dark. Remain hidden and let the light lead you through.

Love is eternal.
X

Jiri sat with his mouth agape. He had read many stories of adventure and even some of terror, but this was not just a story. This was his family. His life.

The afternoon light had already dipped and soon it would be dark. He reached into his pocket and pulled out the notebook. He had so many questions.

So many questions: Three sisters, threads, gods, stars, darkness and light, the one they know as Healy, and he … Jiri was the key.

He stared into space and organised his thoughts until darkness fell. Three questions:

'This isn't real, is it? Is this true?'

Jiri opened the book. Words appeared.

I am sorry, but yes. It is really happening. It is the truth.

'Why.' Jiri said, 'Why not just hide, and let your sisters remain hidden?'

Jiri opened the book again, and he read.

The thread cannot be tied. Not ever.

'But mother. How I can I find them, or warn them? They won't listen to me! I'm not a man like my father!'

You will be.

Jiri watched as his letter began to turn grey. The words he had read started to burn gently and turn to ashes before his eyes.

The other two envelopes remained. Jiri hastily placed the two letters inside the notebook and closed it shut, hard. Tears filled his eyes and as he took the notebook and carried it to his mother's room. He threw it inside and closed the door.

It was too much to take in.

He crumbled with his back against the door, and slowly, gradually, with fits and starts of tears and a whimpering, he slid to the bare wooden floorboards where he remained for a long while.

'I don't want this ... I want my family back.' He ran words around and cried his heart out to the room. Ghosts from his life moved in and out. He remembered his mother dancing about as she cleaned. He remembered his father laughing while he broke the bread at the dining room table. Jiri wanted everything to be the way that it was before.

Before Healy, but Healy was already there in their lives long before he was ever born.

Jiri felt tired. He soon found the strength to stand and walk towards the window where he sat on the ledge. He looked out of the window at the street below. He remembered how his father's car always used to look, strong and present on the side of the road in line with all the other cars.

There was nothing left but a space.

There was nothing left his heart but a hole.

Jiri felt tired, and soon, he dropped to sleep right there on that sill.

In his mother's bedroom, behind that closed door, his father's notebook sat waiting for him.

17

THE IVANOV APARTMENT

LATER THAT NIGHT

Whistling.

Jiri could hear the subtle sound of whistling. As he awoke, he was stunned to find himself on the floor again, but in his grogginess he did not recognise the boards or the apartment.

As Jiri stood he realised. He was inside Mr. Dolya's apartment. The whistling had gotten strong now: Right outside the door.

Whatever the reason for his being there — sleepwalking, or just mere confusion — he recognised the playful tune and couldn't wait to open the door to a familiar and friendly face.

He staggered sleep-drugged to the door, but he

watched as the doorknob was tried on the other side first. Surely if it was Mr. Dolya, he would have had a key and would not try the door — unless he wanted to see if in fact he had forgotten to lock it first.

Of course. That was it, Jiri thought. The idea that he had forgotten to lock the door must have been bothering him all this time he was away.

Jiri looked around and saw the apartment had been ransacked in much the same way as his own. He felt guilty merely for being there in Mr. Dolya's apartment and headed for the window as his only means of leaving as he had done so once before. But the window was shut. He could have opened it, but something told him not to. He felt within his jacket. The cold feeling meant that he didn't have the notebook. He remembered only then that he threw it into his mother's room and had shut the door.

Now he had nowhere to go. Mr. Dolya was still out in the hall and not even trying to open the door.

What if he didn't have a key? Jiri thought and then once again ... he remembered the letter.

What if, I AM THE KEY?

He moved towards the door, slowly, carefully. He stopped, looked around to see that the room was even darker and now, it was empty of any furniture at all.

He turned to the door again and reached for the handle.

I am the key ...

His hand reached into the lock. He felt his hand arrive at the other side of the door and then something touched his fingers.

He pulled his arm back quickly. When he looked down at his hand, it started to crumble and turn to ashes, just like his mother's letter.

Jiri's panic didn't come soon enough. As he held his crumbled arms up in the air, the door swung open. Healy was standing there as if consumed in the darkness of the hallway. He towered above Jiri. Jiri gasped. He let out a scream, but no sound came. He turned back into Mr. Dolya's bare apartment which was consumed with the spread of darkness.

In the corners of the apartment, pairs of cat eyes began to open. He turned his head to another dark area, and more cats opened their eyes to him, wide and green. Wide and green. Along with the vision of more cat eyes came the rising cacophony of growls and snarls.

Jiri felt the warm sensation of a hand on his shoulder. The sensation burnt through his clothing, through his skin.

He turned but the hand was not on his shoulder. Instead, Healy stood there with two heads held up by their hair. Entrails and remnants of spinal bone dripped with blood. Fresh blood.

The heads were recognisable as those of Dax

Shandling, and Nikolai, his own father, both bloated and drooping gormlessly without any muscular tension.

Suddenly Healy stretched his arms out wide. The heads bobbled as they moved outward and then, with a clap of wind, Healy struck the two heads together.

They smashed into what appeared to be a thousand glass shards, maybe more. The glass was ornate and patterned, and every shard that fell sounded like an orchestra of chimes and bells. Each piece glistened with the light of a thousand cat eyes.

In that moment, Jiri awoke.

Jiri was hunched against the inside frame of the windowsill of his own apartment. His neck was stiff and his left arm felt drained and dead — an influence for the subconscious thought. The dream had been left behind in a fog of confused imagery.

It was dark outside, all apart from a car that had pulled in to his father's parking space. He looked out in the night and saw a shadow standing there ... or maybe it was hovering. Jiri inhaled sharply. He snapped back to the car and realised that it was Pavel's.

He quickly shook his arm back to life and ran into his mother's room. He picked up the notebook and stashed it inside his pocket.

At the door, he peered through the peephole. The corridor was dark and quiet. He cupped his ear to hear if anybody was out there, but knew there was only one way to find out to be sure. He couldn't stay in that apartment. He had to get out there even if, by doing so, ran himself into the waiting grasp of Pavel who had clearly come to see if Jiri had returned home.

Mother was right … He thought. It isn't safe … but I'm not going to leave her to this brute …

Quickly, he opened the door and scuttled into the corridor. He could hear the distant footfalls of heavy shoes. Pavel was on his way up.

Jiri ran to Mr. Dolya's door but remembered the dream and was suddenly scared shitless to open it for fear of seeing what was inside.

The notebook was warm against his chest. He looked both ways, down and up the corridor and made his decision.

#

Pavel stood at the end of the corridor. He was tired from his day, but knew he wasn't going to sleep tonight if he didn't check the Ivanov apartment for the fourth time today. He walked up to Mr. Dolya's door and put his ear to it.

'No cats…' he confirmed. 'No bloody cats.'

He touched the scratch at his neck and grumbled some more until he was at the Ivanov apartment. The door was open. He walked on in and announced himself.

'I'm home!' He then snickered. 'Squatters, I'm armed. I haven't shot anybody so far. Don't ruin a near perfect day.'

He checked the main bedroom, and then upon arriving in the living room, he saw the blanket on the floor. He saw the broken box drawer and the curtain rail that lay open ended on the ground.

He looked up and indeed; it was the curtain rail from that room.

'Jiri. Are you still here?' he said as he walked casually, calmly past the kitchenette and to Jiri's bedroom. There was nobody inside. The whole room was a strewn out mess all thanks to his handiwork. 'You know this house is no longer your home. It's pointless coming back. You might as well come home with me. I have a real family. A strong happy family.'

He laughed. Who was he kidding? Jiri wasn't about to fall for that, but Pavel didn't really care what he said. He knew the answer would always be no.

He headed to the main room and looked around and sighed. He checked his gun and walked into the corridor. He looked up and down entire length and decided, perhaps, Jiri was further down, cowering ...

'I know every trick.' He said. 'You can't hide forever.'

#

Jiri was outside, looking up at the window from behind the lamppost. The shadow that was there before had long gone. He had waited long enough and so headed towards Pavel's car, wary and knowing that Pavel would be out of that apartment block within a second.

His plan was to carry on down the road, find someplace new to sleep for the night, but something stopped him at the bonnet.

A feeling.

He saw that the glass from the left bulb; the filament from the tungsten headlamp was smashed whereas the right hand side was intact.

Sure, broken glass was foremost on Jiri's mind, but this was something else. He hadn't had this feeling since he brushed up close to the armchair that he once touched … with memory.

Jiri forgot to check for Pavel for a second, and instead, he wanted to reach out to the broken lamp. His fingers touched the tip of the filament and then everything turned black and silent, and all of a sudden, everything was a dream.

#

Jiri found himself standing on a dark road, miles from anywhere. Light streamed past him. His hand was hot as he moved it away from the brightly lit headlamp of the Skoda that he knew very well.

Ahead in the lights was another car he recognised. His father's car sat at the side of the road. His father was there with his arms at his side. He looked dumb struck as if he had been caught in the act.

No, it was the other way around.

It was his father who had just put two and two together and come to its inevitable conclusion. From behind him, Jiri heard a car door slam shut. Pavel was now standing beside him behind the beam of the car that lit his father up like the angel on a tree.

His father reached for his gun from the inside of his heavy coat pocket, but it was too late. From Jiri's left ear, the shadow of a gun fired off a round. It struck his father right in the chest. He fell to the ground. Jiri screamed out, but no sound ... no sound could be heard.

He tried to move away from where he stood, but he was tied to one spot. His father's gun rose just high enough, but the aim tilted to his left. A gunshot. Jiri saw the headlamp beside him explode and half the light dimmed instantly before his eyes. His father was in darkness. The other side of his car still glistened in the night.

He looked up as Pavel walked onward to his father as he lay on the ground. Nikolai's empty hand reached up, but Pavel had his gun already aimed at his head.

Jiri closed his eyes...

He closed his eyes tight...

He did not want to see it.

He waited.

He waited.

He did not want to see. But he opened his eyes and before his eyes, Healy was there again. This time it was for real. Healy lifted his boot and shunted Jiri to the ground.

#

Jiri lay in the gutter. His feet were in the road and his hands leaned against the curb. His mind was elsewhere. There was no place for tears. He was despondent.

Non-responsive. He sat there staring back and forth at the broken headlamp and then at the road where, in his dreamlike state, his father lay dying. He couldn't do a damn thing about that. But the headlamp was Nikolai's lasting mark on the world.

Jiri saw the doors of the apartment block open. He saw the bulk and swagger of Pavel as he headed out and across the road to his car.

As Pavel arrived at his door, Jiri was already inside, setting down in the dark shadows of the backseat foot well of Pavel's Skoda, out of sight, out of mind.

Jiri felt his blood boil as he smelt the stench of smoke and alcohol and the oil from the grease stained jacket that Pavel simply could not wash off after that night he shot Nikolai. Jiri was barely holding it together. He wanted to tear Pavel apart … and he knew that he could do that right now. He could do anything right now …

But still, Jiri waited until Pavel started the car. Jiri took deep cleansing breaths as he watched Pavel in the reflection of the side mirror as he lit his cigarette. He pinched the cigarette between his lips, reached for his service revolver and placed it on the passenger seat beside him before pulling onto the road.

The car, now in motion, made Jiri's heart beat even faster. Seeing the gun could have sent him over the edge. Jiri wanted so much to do something there and then. His eyes never left that service revolver as Pavel weaved and halted through the evening traffic. Jiri's hands were awash with sweat. He could hear everything in his body pulsing, beating, inhaling, and exhaling. Yet, still, he kept himself quiet and hidden.

Jiri could only see the revolver and the image that confirmed that Pavel had used that weapon to kill his father in cold blood, right there on a darkened country road.

It was then that Jiri wondered: was Healy nearby? Or was Pavel indeed Healy, or vice versa. He did not know anymore.

The notebook was burning against his chest, but he dared not to move an inch. His hand however wanted so much to grab that gun and put it against Pavel's head and blow it through the glass of the driver door. He wanted Pavel to look like more than just a mess. He wanted Pavel to be unrecognisable.

The car stopped.

Pavel tossed out the last of his cigarette and went about removing his gloves, which he placed in the passenger compartment. He reached for his gun ... but it was no longer there on the seat where he'd left it.

Pavel searched his immediate area, but didn't see the service revolver anywhere. He looked on the foot well of the front passenger seat in case it had fallen there and he was ready to begin searching the back seat when somebody tapped on his driver side window.

He opened the door, slowly. His wife was stood there.

'You're late again.' she said, not really that annoyed.

'I had to check something on the way home. It's going to be like that for a while, until we tie everything together.' Pavel padded down his own jacket. 'I can't seem to find my service revolver. I know I had it ...'

'Just come inside. The children stayed up just for you. They have a surprise for you!' The sound of her voice faded and Pavel grumbled and stepped out of the vehicle.

'I know I had it — ' he said as his voice faded away from the car. He sounded different from any other time. Jiri knew him as the brute, the force, the heavyweight monster, but here, in his home he was obedient, distilled ... calm and filtered.

A family man: and Jiri listened until he heard the front door of Pavel's townhouse shut tight behind him.

A family man: something Jiri's family could be no more. Jiri left the car behind and started to walk towards Pavel's grand white townhouse. It had five windows to five separate rooms. Indeed, Pavel had done well for himself.

Very well for himself ...

Jiri stood at his window, staring through into the room, he saw Pavel as he picked up his young boy – a mere toddler. Pavel was then enthusiastically dragged over to see something handmade by his older daughter who was shy of her junior years. Jiri was confused. Pavel wasn't this. He was nothing of the kind, but yet, the reality did not tell a lie. Pavel was not the monster Jiri wanted him to be. Jiri was every bit the monster who now stood gazing into his life, holding a service revolver in his hand with the burning desire to kill. Before him was a scene of peace and civility. It was not perfect ... but it was damn close to being just that.

Jiri felt the heat from inside his jacket pocket. He knew it was his mother. She was sending a message to him, but he didn't need to read the notebook to know what it was she was going to say.

#

Pavel heard the doorbell ring. He put down his daughter who playfully clung to his leg all the way to his hallway. He was stern but fair as he told her to "run along" as he walked across to open the door.

Who could it be at this time of night? It was not a time for work to come knocking. He grumbled and then, worked out quickly in his head what it was he was going to say to the StB officer who was about to insist he join him at yet another crime scene.

Not tonight, he thought. I have to rest. It can wait.

He opened the door and assumed the stature of a brute to whoever was ready to announce his request for Pavel to join him for more twilight adventures in the seedy underworld of Czechoslovakia.

But there was nobody there.

He looked left, and right, and stepped out a little, cautious now that he was being taunted by one of the neighbourhood children. It looked like another session of "knock & run" and he was dead set against rising to the bait. He was ready to walk away and close the door when he noticed his service revolver sat cold and still on the welcome mat at his feet.

Pavel's mouth dropped. He picked it up, but didn't want to announce that he'd found it just yet.

It was too convenient. It was too much of a coincidence. But stranger still, one thing was for sure.

Guns don't ring doorbells.

18

PRAGUE CENTRAL STATION

NIGHT

> "I know you won't want to leave, but I am telling you, as a mother to her son whom she loves more than life itself ... leave Prague."

Jiri needed only to ask his mother, hand on notebook, what he should do. If settling a score with Pavel was not it, then what was it?

The notebook felt warm and he read inside the pages an almost exact copy of Patricia's letter to Jiri. He wasn't going to be allowed to forget what was asked of him. There really was no reason to stick around. Pavel would find him, eventually, and then what?

> "Leave Prague, and head to Boston, England, which is where the second sister was sent. Leave Prague."

The smell of the train station was unmistakable. A deep dark taste of industry carried weight, and Jiri only had to follow his nose to find the grand structure with its twin fat turrets and its massive roof structure that were black with smoke and soot. In the darkness of night, there were very few passengers. With no money and very little chance of getting on board through means of charity, good will, or the powers of persuasion, Jiri went about looking for a train.

But which one?

There were three trains at present at the main terminal. Further along were other platforms that were disconnected from the mainline (a thread through to other places). Police and passport control heavily guarded the far end of the platform. Not every line was guarded.

He quickly found a bench where a family sat waiting; mother, and a father and two girls, all of whom sat with suitcases of their own. The youngest girl sat with a doll in a stroller. She didn't fuss with the doll. It just sat there, staring up with painted eyes that reminded Jiri of the masks that his mother made.

Sitting next to the doll stroller was a good plan.

He was far enough from the family not to intrude on their privacy, but close enough to not stand out as being a loner. He wanted to know where they were going, see if his tagging along was for the long haul, but it wasn't a good feeling to ask outright.

He held the notebook in his hand and asked quietly in his mind. Where do I need to go? Which train?

He opened the book and saw nothing.

It didn't work.

He shrugged, closed the book and tried again.

Where do I need to go? Please ... tell me which train I need to find?

This time, he felt the notebook throb and get warm under his hands. Being that this gave the added benefit of warmth, he waited until the book cooled before opening.

Perhaps that was the secret, because this time, as clear as day, a word appeared on one of the later pages of the notebook.

Travel directly to East Berlin, East Germany.

Do not attempt to get a train until you walk to the West Berlin terminal.

Then get a train to Bonn, West Germany.

Then to Rotterdam, Holland.

Boat or freight ship to Boston, Lincolnshire, England

Jiri nodded and thanked his mother. He smiled, not because he had the message he hoped for, but that he was sure that in those words he heard both his mother and father speaking. His father was always about directions, and Patricia, precautions.

Now with that information set, he stood from the bench leaving behind his theoretical family who sat waiting for their train, and went to look at the trains for signs marking out destinations.

He at first assumed he would find such information from the boards or passing train guards but they simply weren't about at this time of night. There were several old-school steam stokers and a bunch of track maintenance men, all chuffing harder on their smokes with more vigour than that of the diesel trains they took care of. None of them made eye contact. All were tired and not approachable.

The only reliable source of information would come from the train drivers and any staff that might be on board.

Jiri scouted the platform and found, further along the terminal, the path where the police presence was weakest. What the difference was, Jiri had no idea.

It was then that he heard whistling. The tune was Pop Goes the Weasel. The same tune that was whistled by Mr. Dolya, there was no doubt. Jiri looked about expectantly. Of course, it had to be Mr. Dolya. Naivety be damned, for nobody else would dare whistle inside a building at night, and certainly not such a joyous tune such as Pop Goes the Weasel.

He followed the whistling and skidded to a halt, as he found the man who sat in a brown raincoat and a matching brown fedora with an orange silk lining. He looked at him for a moment, not recognising the elements, the silhouette that identified his good neighbour. Indeed, as the man lifted his head, Jiri realised he was not the man he knew at all.

As the two locked eyes, the whistling stopped. Jiri searched for a reason to say something, anything to the man who was clearly sat there waiting for his train to arrive. He carried nothing more than an attaché case, which rested on his lap.

Jiri didn't have to say anything, so it seemed, the man was ready to talk first.

'It's past your curfew.' The man said. His voice was strangely familiar to Jiri. At ease Jiri approached the man and waited at the bench end to talk away from sight of the main walk through to all the various platforms.

'I'm with my family.'

'Perhaps, you should go sit with them...'

'They're waiting for a train.' Jiri thought on his feet. 'Which one are you waiting for?'

The man who whistled thought for a moment

before answering.

'Why would you want to know that?'

'I'm just looking for our platform.' Jiri answered. 'I just thought — '

The man who whistled interrupted.

'You thought you'd come and ask me where I was heading, so you could hopefully find commonality, and therefore find your platform which your family should already know, because they already bought a ticket.'

'Yes... I'm just trying to have a bit of fun while I wait.'

The man laughed.

'Where are you going, boy? He asked.

Jiri thought. 'Berlin.'

'Everybody is going to Berlin, Jiri, but the real question would be, where are you escaping from?'

Jiri dipped his head, thought for a moment, 'I'm travelling with family.'

'You don't have to pretend.' The stranger said. 'I saw you arrive. I've watched you as you wander. You're a lone traveller without a clue about where, or how. Perhaps I can help?'

Jiri lifted his head. Not only could this stranger whistle like Mr. Dolya but also he was as smart as Mr. Dolya along with it. He spoke a compassionate tone.

'Jiri, you have to understand that if you're heading west, through that so-called iron curtain, you will need all the help you can get. Are you going west?'

'I think so. To England.'

'Then yes, you will have to pass through the iron curtain.'

Jiri looked around. He hadn't seen any curtains, just a heavy police presence on certain platforms.

'You look confused.'

'Where do I find the iron curtain?'

The stranger laughed. Gestured to Jiri, 'Take a seat.'

The stranger opened his case and showed Jiri a timetable complete with a crudely drawn map of the current state of the countries that surrounded them.

'Your education is lacking, young boy. Perhaps they've filled you with the rising influences of the Marxist-Leninist doctrine that has clouded your reality. You can't just go to England from here. You have to go to Berlin first.'

'That's what my mother told me to do.'

The stranger raised an eyebrow. 'Your mother is sending you to England. I suppose you have family there?'

'That's right. My aunt. I'm going to find her.'

'Well, isn't that something.' The stranger drew a very long deep breath before running his finger along a red line on his map that split the countries apart from one another. 'You will definitely have to get to Berlin first. You see, it is the only city along the "Iron Curtain divide" that is represented by all sides. I've heard they're thinking of remedying that by building a wall. As if a wall will make the world a better place.' He laughed, more to himself than to Jiri. 'But anyway, this is your lucky day. I can help you get on that train, no questions asked. It'll cost you though.'

Jiri shook his head.

'I don't have any money.'

'You don't?' The stranger choked on his ice-cold breath. 'Well then that's going to make things difficult.' He then smiled. 'Perhaps I'm feeling charitable today. I will still help you, because I can see in your eyes that you need this more than I could ever know.'

'Yes sir.' Jiri perked up. 'I do.'

The stranger retrieved from his case, a pass of some kind and closed the latches. He stood and gestured that Jiri should stand also.

'What is your name?' he asked

'Jiri.'

'Just Jiri?' the stranger asked.

Jiri thought a moment and realised that the name Ivanov had been dragged through the mud as of late, and so stated clearly.

'Just Jiri.' He said. And in that moment, the notebook within his inside pocket began to throb. He felt it, but knew he couldn't get it out now. He decided he would wait until he was on the train, safe and en route to Berlin.

'Stay close, Just Jiri.' They walked along the platforms towards one of the great diesel trains that had more carriages attached to its front than was possible to see from this viewpoint at the station.

The Gathering Thread

The man walked with Jiri through several checkpoints. Police saw as the man flashed a card and there were no questions asked. They carried on through. Jiri felt invincible.

'You won't have to hide on this train. It's direct, no stops. You won't need a ticket. I'll take care of everything.' The stranger said.

Music to Jiri's ears.

The notebook was throbbing, but it was still not the time to retrieve it.

'I won't have to hide?'

'Perhaps when you get to Berlin you will need to use discretion; from that point on you won't have my help. You will be on your own. Is that okay with you?'

'Oh yes, sir. Thank you, sir.' Jiri was grateful.

They walked along the longest train Jiri had ever seen. He didn't even care to count how many carriages there were. Most of the train was comprised of compartments. They climbed on in and headed into a compartment that was empty.

'Sit here, Jiri, and wait until I get back.' At the door to the compartment, he said, 'I would like to offer a suggestion. Change your name. Jiri is clearly from the wrong side and you'll be on a train back to Prague in no time. Might I suggest, Nicholas.'

He closed the door to the compartment and walked down the carriage. Jiri was perplexed. Nicholas sounded like his father's name.

Did this man know his father?

Who was this stranger?

Jiri watched in awe as the signalman on the platform ordered the train doors closed and soon Jiri felt at ease. He saw several others walk down the corridor speaking German.

A good sign.

Behind the platform was another train. He saw the baby doll in the stroller, along with the two girls and their parents, all getting checked before boarding. A policeman took out the doll and pulled back the covers, and immediately the father of the family was arrested. Jiri was aghast as reams of papers were retrieved from the little girls' toy stroller. There was a lot of yelling. Money spilled from the stroller as well as other items that Jiri couldn't identify. The mother held on to the children, but as soon as other police officers came their way, she too was arrested and the children were forced away from their parents.

The whole platform began to move, and it was then that Jiri noticed the stranger was standing on the platform, talking to several Soviet police officers. They looked onward, towards the family, shaking their heads at the unfortunate situation that had unravelled before their eyes.

The stranger noticed the train was finally moving and looked Jiri in the eye. He smiled, waved, and then turned away.

He didn't look like Mr. Dolya, Jiri thought as he noticed the platform was still moving on ...

Jiri suddenly twigged: It wasn't the platform. It was him that was moving. Jiri pressed himself against the glass, banged his fists, and tried to let the stranger know that he was supposed to be there with him. He was supposed to be with him on that train all the way to Berlin.

Jiri panicked. He sat down quickly, reached into his jacket, and retrieved the notebook.

He opened it and leafed through until he found a page where words had indeed appeared.

Only a few words were needed; words that Jiri could not believe.

Jiri. You're on the wrong train!

On the platform, the stranger watched as Jiri's train sped away towards the open rail, beyond the station and bound for Moscow. He sighed in relief. That one was too easy. He looked to the Soviet officer who passed him a cigarette.

'How many strays is that for you tonight?' the Soviet officer said.

'Only one this time.' the stranger said. 'It's a slow, slow night.'

He took a long drag from the cigarette and waited for Jiri's train to finally disappear from sight.

To Be Continued…

ABOUT THE AUTHOR

Stephen is a prolific storyteller, writing across many venues and forms; including feature and short screenwriting, radio plays and commercial radio, short story, article writing, and music. He is also a voice artist for audio books. Stephen is the host for the interview based podcast, *Headline This*, and co-host of the humour filled film analysis podcast, *Frame By Frame*. He writes a regular blog, *Film in Light & Motion*, where he overindulges in the details of film and other creative mediums.

The *Threads of Fate* trilogy has proved to be a departure from the familiar genre of science fiction, of which Stephen has many world building projects lined up for future publication.

Stephen lives in Manchester with his wife, two sons and two cats – the latter being his biggest critics. *The Gathering Thread* is book one in the *Threads of Fate* trilogy, and is Stephen's first published work.

Website: http://stephenradford.com

Twitter: @ StephenPRadford

Printed in Great Britain
by Amazon